THE SAGA
OF
DANNY JONES

A JOURNEY TO NEW BEGINNINGS

BARBARA CAMPBELL MCLAWHORN

I dedicate this book to my family members for their encouragement and unwavering support. This book is also dedicated to the thousands of young people I had the honor of serving throughout my 28 years as a teacher and school counselor.

CHAPTER ONE

FIRST DAY OF SUMMER BREAK

It was Saturday morning and the beginning of my summer break from school. I was promoted to the tenth grade and was excited about the thought of no longer being teased by the upperclassmen about being a freshman. I had achieved sophomore status and it felt great. Earlier this morning at about 2:00 a.m., my mom, Olivia Jones, received a high alert phone call from Sullivan Hospital asking her to report to work ASAP. Sullivan is where she is employed as a nurse anesthetist and it's located just outside of Philadelphia. She was informed that several people were in need of emergency surgery as the result of a big brawl at a local hangout.

Mom had been gone for several hours and my dad, Daniel Jones, was in the kitchen preparing breakfast for my nine-year-old sister, Marissa (whom I call Lil' Sis), and me. He called for me to get up and make a run to the corner store to buy a quart of orange juice and a loaf of whole wheat bread. I was tired and didn't feel like moving. All I wanted to do was relax and enjoy not being in a regimen of getting up early. A few minutes later, I heard my dad saying, "Everything is almost ready and I see that the money is still down here on the mantel. Let's get it going, Danny." Knowing my dad, I knew that was considered my second warning and that there wouldn't be a third.

While lying in bed, I began to stretch and the thought of having to get up didn't sit well with me. However, I rolled out of bed and got prepared to go to Old Man John's corner store. First, I walked past a few houses and then I broke out into a superfast run. I was running hard and fast so I could get past Miss Bertha Mae Brown's house without having to stop and engage in one of her long daily conversations. My main goal was to return home and get back in my bed. It felt like my feet were on fire. Believe me, if I were at a track meet, I would have won a royal blue ribbon, trimmed in pure gold with my name spelled out in real diamonds.

I was getting in gear to run past Miss Bertha Mae Brown's house when I heard a familiar voice saying, "Now, wait a minute here, young man, hold your horses. Don't you dare run past me and not speak. Don't you remember our conversation yesterday about somebody always having their eyes on you? I saw you as soon as you stepped foot out your front door, then when you displayed your God-given athletic ability a few houses down the street from mine, determined to run past me without speaking. Oh please, saying good morning does not hurt anyone. Some people take the time to speak to animals they don't even know, like you did yesterday when you showed compassion for that little black and white stray dog wandering the streets. I had just sent the little Thomas twins, Barry and Gary, home for being abusive to that little dog. Then, you came along and I felt an abundance of pride when I heard you say, 'Hi, little buddy, what's up?' It was heartwarming to see how kind you were to him and then to see it follow you down the street. But this morning to me, someone made in the image of God, as we all are, you said absolutely nothing, trying to zip on past me without speaking. I've also found, especially with the younger people nowadays, Danny, words like 'thank you,' 'please,' or 'excuse me' are not used too often in their conversations. When I talk to some of them, I get no response at all, which causes me to wonder if this new generation has severe hearing loss or perhaps, unfortunately, poor home training. Some of them even go through a door and let it slam in the face of the person directly behind them. And now, here you go, trying your best to run past me without speaking."

Miss Bertha Mae continued. "It is well known that you can catch more flies with honey than you can with vinegar."

I was confused, and in a hurry, so I said, "Flies, why would I want to catch flies? That doesn't even make any sense. You must be losing your mind if you think for one second that I want to catch flies. That's one of the most ludicrous things I've ever heard. I'll tell you what, if you want to catch flies, then I suggest that you get yourself a jar of honey, or better yet, a can of Raid Flying Insect Spray so you can have a field day catching all the flies you want." I became fed up and began to mimic her words under my breath, then showed her a quick fake smile followed by a fake laugh.

Miss Bertha Mae Brown replied, "I see you don't quite understand what I am saying today. You are taking what I said literally rather than figuratively. There is a great message in that saying, young man, and the people who abide by it are usually more successful in life than those who don't. But, if you do not, you'll understand it better as time passes on." She then pivoted the conversation and said, "But, if you really want to know now what it means, then I suggest that you have a little talk with your parents and I'm sure they will help you have a clearer understanding."

When I got home, I ran part of the conversation past my dad. Even though Miss Bertha Mae had been talking off the chain and in rare form, a few of her words jolted my interest immensely. I was curious about the flies, the honey, and the vinegar thing, and since my dad is a zoologist, I wanted to hear what he had to say. I told him that Miss Bertha Mae had been talking some crazy ol' talk today. I explained to him that I could hardly believe she was talking to me about some flies and how I can catch more of them with honey than I can with vinegar. I did not have enough time to listen to her rambling nonsense that went on and on, so I left and went to the store.

My dad looked at me and calmly said, "Sit down here at the table, son. We need to have a little talk." He asked what had occurred to spark the conversation about the flies, the honey, and the vinegar.

At his request, I freely divulged everything, because I knew if I didn't, and if he asked Miss Bertha Mae, she would surely fill in all the missing blanks. I thought it would be less upsetting if he heard it from me first. So, being that I thought he would be in agreement with what I was about to say, I laid it all out like a detailed blueprint.

I said, "Dad, that old woman is nerve-wracking and I am tired of her saying something to me every time I go past her old dilapidated house, with her sitting up there looking out of that second-floor window. She looks like an old character that just stepped out of a history book. And if she's not there, then an old song called 'Jesus Is Love,' recorded many years ago before I was even born, by Lionel Richie and the Commodores, fills the air as it flows out from her window to the street. She plays that same song over and over again. It has to be on a loop. My friends and I know all of the words to it. I've heard it so much, sometimes I find myself humming it for no apparent reason. Why can't she get with it and play something else? That woman is so out of touch. She still uses a flip phone and probably does not know anything about computers. I would be shocked if she knew how to turn one on and even more astonished if she could use it. Remember the microwave ovens the church gave to the elderly for Christmas three years ago, to help make meal preparation easier? Well, I remember her thank-you note to the church said 'Thanks a Million' for remembering her during the Christmas season. That same microwave is still in the original box sitting on her kitchen counter. The seal has never been broken. It seems like she just can't relate to modem technology and everything that's happening. Her mind is back there somewhere in the old-school days, always telling me about how things used to be. Who cares about how, as a child, she would ride to church in a horse and buggy? Not me. I don't want to hear anything else about all of that mess from the past. I live in the present and I'm jetting towards the future. To-day, her telling me that old ridiculous story about flies, honey, and vinegar was a bit too much. You know what, Dad, it might be time for her to take up permanent residence somewhere else, like at the old folks' home where she can knit, play bingo and checkers all day long, and stop getting on my case. I've had enough of her."

My dad and I have always had a good father-and-son relationship. He is known to be a pretty fair guy, but, after I finished venting about Miss Bertha Mae Brown, I looked at him, thinking he was going to be on my side and ready to go down the street to her house to tell her to get off my case. Boy, oh boy, oh boy was I ever wrong. He looked blown away. I could see that he was all hot and flustered under his collar—not at Miss Bertha Mae, but, surprisingly, at me. I knew immediately that I had stepped in some deep, bad-smelling stuff when he asked what had happened to my self-control today, and most importantly, who had appointed me judge and jury? It was as clear as day that I was not going to get away with my antics this time. He was not at all pleased with me.

He looked at me and raised his voice saying, "When did you become so pompous and develop all of that sinful hate in your heart?" He said, in life, some people may have ways we do not understand or we just don't like, but even with all of that, there is never a good reason to lower yourself to be disrespectful to anyone, especially to the elderly. They've paved the way for us and now, as we proudly stand high upon their shoulders, we should be appreciative and thankful for all that they have done, making sacrifices so that we can have a better life. I've never seen my dad look like that in my entire life. He looked genuinely hurt, distraught, and expressed a profound disappointment in my behavior. He was all over my case like white on rice. He said to me, "When your mother gets home, we're going to have a family meeting and pray to God for His guidance in developing a plan of action that will help you have a better understanding and appreciation for those you may perceive as not being worthy of your respect. When I was a child, I was told not to be critical of anyone, because as I criticized others, they too, could feel the exact same way about me. Your theatrical shenanigans will not be tolerated. God chose me to be your earthly father, and with that honor comes a tremendous responsibility. I refuse to be negligent in fulfilling my duty as your dad. I don't know what has gotten into you lately to cause you to think you are superior to anyone. You are an extension of your mother and me and you were not reared that way. Mark my words, Danny boy, a change is going to come. It's time for you to be brought back to reality for your own sake."

Dad said he clearly understood the meaning of a phrase that contained the words "flies," "honey," and "vinegar" and that no other words were necessary. Dad further explained, "When someone uses the words 'flies,' 'honey,' and 'vinegar' in the same sentence about you, that's an old way of telling you indirectly that you have been very disrespectful. You can't get very far in life hating on others. This type of behavior is unacceptable." In the meantime, he said, there would be no social media or any other type of artificial intelligence in my life. He stomped his size 12W shoe hard on the floor and said, "Shut down the gadgets, all of them, right now!" I thought, *Oh man! I just got a new phone two days ago!*

When my mom returned home from work and heard about my exchange of words with Miss Bertha

Mae, one thing was for sure: the heat was on. She turned it way up.

My mom, normally a very calm and gentle person, rose quickly to the occasion at hand and stated, "You've got to get yourself together, son, for good manners will freely open up doors of success that poor behavior cannot pry open, even with a crowbar. It's the same principle as 'you reap what you sow.' If you want strawberries, then surely you wouldn't sow rutabaga turnip seeds because that's exactly what you will get: rutabaga turnips."

Mom continued. "We know, unfortunately, that you had a trying first year in high school after being so involved in middle school, and are now trying to find out where you fit in the grand scheme of things. We understand, and that's a part of life. It's called growing up. What we want you to realize, however, is that your negative behavior affects not only you, but our entire family. I felt hurt when your history teacher called to say that you had been cutting class, and almost floored a few weeks ago when the assistant principal called about you being suspended for three days for fighting, then demanded that I come immediately to take you off the school grounds. Most challenges, depending on how you handle them, can make you a better and stronger person. Your dad and I were hoping that this summer break from school would give you a chance to regroup and develop a sense of belonging when it's time to go back in the fall. But today, you really crossed the line. What we don't understand, however, is what made you think that you can be so rude to anyone, especially our elderly neighbor Miss Bertha Mae Brown of all people."

We had our family meeting, and after much discussion, my parents agreed that I needed to spend more time with people advanced in their senior years. Mom said that I needed to become familiar with what David said in Psalm 71:9 in the King James Version of the Bible about the treatment of the elderly: "Cast me not off in the time of old age, forsake me not when my strength faileth." She said if I did Miss Bertha Mae Brown like that, she cringed at the thought of who I would be disrespectful to next.

At the conclusion of our meeting, my parents agreed that such behavior must not be allowed to continue. A few phone calls were made by my dad, while Mom swiftly packed my clothes in a duffle bag, and gave me a bag lunch with two fried bologna and cheese sandwiches, two peanut butter and jelly sandwiches, an apple, a large bag of chips, and a large drink. In addition, she packed my Bible, which had been sitting in my bedroom on the top of my bookshelf collecting dust. Her words to me were "Son, this is your rock, don't leave home without it." Dad gave me a few dollars for pocket money, drove me straight to the Greyhound Bus Station, and bought me a one-way ticket on the first bus headed to Marion County, South Carolina.

Marion County is where my paternal grandmother lives. Her name is Bretta Jones, but I call her Granny. Some people refer to Marion County as the sticks, while others call it the boondocks, and still another group calls it home sweet home. To me, it's a nightmare in the middle of the woods, with no Wi-Fi, where there is nothing to do but sit around and listen to crickets chirping, mosquitoes buzzing, roosters crowing, and a lot of bloodsucking insects doing their thing. The lack of meaningful activities is probably why so many people leave that area after high school and don't return. Since there is nothing to do around there, I thought I would finally get a chance to spend my time lounging around and catching up on my rest. No one lives at my Granny's house but her; therefore, I figured, I'd have a peaceful stay with no one to bother me.

My dad made it crystal clear that the money he set aside as a donation to help troubled teens was being spent for my bus ticket. "Evidently," he said, "I have one right here under my nose, in my own house, and didn't even know the severity of it." My dad, who is a believer in taking care of family first, said that my behavior needed to be put in check. In addition, he said, this worthwhile investment in my life was his desire to stop me from making down payments on a one-way ticket to a place I'd never heard of before; he called it "Abyss." I looked at my mom and then at my dad, hoping to change either or both of their minds. But, one thing was for sure, they weren't going to cave and were in lockstep with each other.

Dad continued. "It is clear that you are in need of an intervention and your mother and I are here to support you. At the rate you are going, if a change doesn't occur in a few years, we might have to tag your luggage not only to Abyss, but all the way down to the South Abyss Station."

My mom said, "We love you, Danny, and wish you only the best; however, we are very concerned about your actions towards Miss Bertha Mae and about how you may be disrespecting others. Rest assured, this type of behavior must be nipped in the bud. You're getting out of control and it's time for you to go." I felt strange because

I'd never been put out of anywhere before in my life—except for that three-day suspension from school—and here were my parents putting me out of the house and telling me that I had to hit the road.

My dad concluded by stating, "You have great potential and a bright future ahead of you, son. We want you to learn and use the many talents you received from God to help make you a complete and successful person. That is why we believe it is time for you to get on the bus to take the journey of absolution for at least a few weeks."

CHAPTER TWO

THE BUS RIDE

The beginning of my adventure started at 3:00 p.m. with a bus ride down to my Granny Bretta Jones's house. It was a long and tedious ride. The bus made frequent stops as people got on and off at their destinations. Some of them were very friendly, while others were not. Some of the passengers wouldn't even look at you, let alone speak. They kept their focus on finding a seat, then flopping down, appearing exhausted. One man was overly friendly and just would not stop talking. When he walked down the aisle, he gave high fives to some of the passengers, while others shouted out insults at him. One of them started singing an old song that my dad has in his outdated collection of tapes called "Funky Broadway." He was surrounded by his own funky funk and the smell of his breath was atrocious. His tennis shoes reeked a smell of pure stank, probably accumulated from many years past to the present. To add insult to it all, he intermittently spewed out loud, sour-smelling burps that sounded like a trombone, followed by him sophisticatedly saying, "Pardon me, please." He then flopped down beside me. I was thankful his problem was coming from his upper body rather than the lower. Some of the passengers, sitting near my seatmate and me, became upset about his odor and insisted that the driver throw him off the bus.

The bus driver's answer to that request was "Everybody and anybody gets to ride this bus. He has a ticket to ride and that's what he's going to do. He is just as entitled to ride this bus as anyone else. So, stop complaining and get over it." At this time, a very small elderly lady made her way back to our seat and politely said that she was a retired registered nurse and has a similar problem and that she takes an over-the-counter medicine that has been helpful for her.

"Hopefully," she said, "these will give you some relief," as she handed him an antacid. "Please go to your doctors for help; that is, your medical doctor and your spiritual doctor. They will see you through your problems. The ball is in your court, it is up to you to take care of yourself."

As soon as the gentle-sounding lady, who was holding on to the backs of seats and taking short steps to keep her balance, made it back to her seat and sat down, "Mr. Broadway" got up and pulled down his clanking-sounding backpack from the overhead rack and offered me a taste of his prized possessions. He had two bottles of Mad Dog 20/20. One bottle was half empty.

He looked at me and said, "You look like you had a hard day, boy, take a swallow from either one of the bottles. I don't mind. It will help you to relax and forget about all of your miseries. It will make you feel better and it tastes oh, so good."

I said, "No, thanks," then pretended to fall asleep, with my left eye closed and my right eyelid slightly ajar. To my surprise, he screwed one cap off, then screwed it back on and did not take a drink from either bottle, but returned his backpack to the overhead rack. I wondered if that little talk with that caring elderly lady made a difference. One thing I must say about this good-natured drunken man is he, or someone he knows, was smart to get him on that bus, funk and all. Whew! After all, it was just a temporary inconvenience for some of us, and perhaps a lifesaving decision for others. A couple of months ago, my dad's car was hit by a drunk driver. Everybody in the car came out alright except for Lil' Sis. A hard impact was made on the side of the car where she was sitting and it badly injured her right leg. Even though a lot of time has passed, it continues to bother her. I wish that drunk driver had not gotten behind the wheel of that car and inflicted that pain on my little sister.

We continued on our way, headed for the Deep South. I sat there as thoughts continued to race through my mind. Was what I said so vile that I had to be separated from my family and friends? My parents constantly say that I'm growing like a weed, and consequently outgrowing my senses. What does that mean anyway? It doesn't sound like anything good, that's for sure. That old Miss Bertha Mae Brown is always minding someone else's business. I was on this bus just because of her. She always had something to say about everything. Then she'd turn right around and ask me to do things for her, like move her trash cans back from the curb or go to the corner store to pick up things for her like she was entitled because she's old. This should've been her seat on this bus, not mine. It was almost time for football conditioning to start, and here I sat, on my way to the sticks, just because of her. The thought of her made my stomach churn and I was beginning to feel nauseous. I needed to be out there on the football field to show the coach what I could do.

The next stop was Alexandria, Virginia. This was the stop for my seatmate to get off the bus. He stood up, stretched, and reached for his bag of goodies.

He said, "I don't know why you're on this bus heading south, fellow, but I do know what it meant when I was a child. It meant that somebody had gotten too big for his britches and needed a wise person to talk or knock some common sense back into his head. Many of my friends took this same type of trip and turned out well and became very successful people. I laughed at them when they left. Back in the day, I wish my parents had cared enough to have sought out some special help for me. Perhaps I would have had a better life and it would have kept me from being full of misery and shame. I thought I had it made. Nobody could tell me anything. I thought I knew it all—and then some—only to learn later in life that I didn't and the joke was strictly on me. I did whatever I wanted to do. When I was younger, my friends were all envious of me because of my parents' hands-off approach in my rearing. I looked back over the years and concluded that slack parents either don't care enough about their children and their future or they lacked parenting skills. If they did care, they would correct them while they are young and eliminate the possibility of repeated heartbreaking offenses. It's like a young sapling tree which can be trained to grow in different shapes while it's young, but if you wait too long, it grows and becomes hard and uncontrollable. I wish a mentor had stepped in and helped me out during the void left by my too lenient parents. That's enough about me and my past. I'm looking forward to a new day and starting fresh. First, I'm getting counseling for myself and then I'm extending a helping hand to others, for they say that God helps those who help themselves and that "faith without works is dead" (James 2:26). Dude, maybe I misread your story or maybe I didn't, but whatever reason caused you to be on this bus, I wish you Godspeed."

I said thank you and he exited through the back door of the bus. My seatmate was now gone, but his words continued to linger just like the smell of his funky funk. I shall never forget him.

Soon, the bus was on its way to another designation somewhere deep in the state of Virginia. This time a crying baby and his mother, along with three little siblings, got on board. Even though there were some vacant seats where they could have spread out to have more room, the mother guided them to the seat where she was going to sit. The children sat down towards the window and the mother sat in the aisle seat, giving off the vibe that she was her children's protector and on duty. Soon the passengers were settled in and ready to go. The baby started in with a loud, shrill cry that made most of us irritable because it was late and we wanted to go to sleep. However, the crying baby made it known that he was in charge and he cried as long as he wanted to cry.

Some passengers shouted, "Hush up that crying baby" and one lady said, "Please be patient; patience is a virtue. Besides, a crying baby is evidence that life continues to thrive." The bus left the station and traveled a few miles down the road. The baby stopped crying, probably due to the vibrating movement of the bus. Finally, we got what we longed for: peace and quiet.

When we reached North Carolina, some passengers got off and others got on. Luckily, no one needed to sit next to me this time so this was my chance to have more space to rest. The wheels on the bus kept on rolling. It passed through large cities, small towns, and hamlets. We also traveled through long stretches of nothing but trees, especially pines, as we got closer to my destination in the county of Marion, South Carolina. The bus driver got on his loudspeaker and said, "Our next stop will be the town of Mullins, known for uh, uh, uh, I don't know, but I challenge you to put it on the map for something good and I wish you well."

The bus driver let me off at a closed gas station at around 4:00 a.m. with only one streetlight in sight. It was very dark with only a few stars aglow. There waiting for me, all by herself, was my grandma, Bretta Jones, with her arms stretched wide open, ready to greet me. She hugged me and said, "Welcome, baby, I'm so glad you are here."

We headed to her car. Then, I turned to wave goodbye to the bus driver and there was nothing there. The bus, the driver, and the remaining passengers were all gone in what seemed like a flash. The bus seemed to have literally vanished into thin air. *What's going on?* I wondered if I was daydreaming or perhaps in a trance. I rode on that bus for thirteen hours and now it was gone, a thing of the past. I continued to challenge myself to find a tangible explanation for what happened to the bus, but did not come up with a reasonable answer. It was all a mystery to me. What had just happened? I thought of what I learned in school about the effect of secondhand smoke on the nonsmoker. Could this possibly also be true for someone who does not drink alcohol but takes in the fumes that escape from the pores and breath of an alcoholic's body? If so, I thought, I'm doomed. Granny and I talked about my experience and she told me to clear my head, get a good night's sleep, and not to lean on my own understanding.

Just as I was settling in to a deep sleep, Granny knocked on my door and stated that she was leaving for church. She encouraged me to catch up on my rest and that she would see me after church. I spent most of the day resting.

CHAPTER THREE

DOWN ON THE FARM

Monday

The next morning, I was awakened by the smell of fried bacon, eggs, stone-ground grits, and freshly baked big fluffy buttermilk biscuits. I wanted to get up to eat, but my body was still exhausted after that long ride and it did not want to cooperate. So, I lay in bed and stretched and stretched. Granny called for me to come to the table. Magically, my feet hit the floor and I headed to the small kitchen. Everybody knows you don't keep my grandma waiting.

First, she said, "Good morning, baby."

I responded, "Good morning, Granny." She was so excited about me visiting her that she opened a fresh jar of her prizewinning local honey to be eaten with her famous homemade hot buttermilk biscuits.

She said, "Eat all you want, Danny. There is a lot of work to be done around here today. Eat well so you can keep up your strength." She said that she let her hired help take a break for a few weeks so that she could spend as much time as possible with me and felt that the two of us could handle the daily chores around her small farm together.

The delicious breakfast was the last good thing I remember about that day.

Sweet Grandma had me working extremely hard. I worked so hard until I honestly thanked my Heavenly Father for creating me with automatic breathing because, otherwise, I might have forgotten to breathe several times during that day. My first assignment was to wash all of the windows in the house inside and out with a vinegar and herb solution Granny concocted. It had a disturbingly strong smell. It was so strong, it opened up my sinus cavities—I had some serious draining going on. It's hard cleaning windows and trying to keep your nose clean at the same time. Next, I swept the pine straw off the roof of the house, cut the grass, then raked the yard, front and back. Just as I thought I could take a break, Granny reminded me that the chickens needed feeding and the hogs needed to be slopped. First, I fed the chickens. While they were up eating, I collected the eggs. I was surprised to see the difference in the color of the eggs and their sizes. They ranged from small to jumbo. There were a lot of white eggs and some brown eggs. I was familiar with all of that, but the surprise came when I saw the pretty, natural pastel colors of the blue eggs and eggs of pale green. They were a sight to behold. When I went inside to put the eggs in the refrigerator, I had a conversation with Granny about the differences.

She explained, "When they're all cracked, scrambled, and fried up, they look and taste the same." She asked if I knew the colors of the eggs I had eaten that morning for breakfast and I said "no, ma'am." She said that she could not remember either because she just reached in the egg tray and began to crack eggs because she knew they would all taste the same. She said, "The outsides may look different, but what really matter is what's inside." I thought to myself, "I've heard that type of reasoning before," then I went back outside to do the rest of my chores.

I completed all the chores that Granny assigned me to do. Then she came outside to tell me that the mule didn't have any water in his trough. All I could think was "my Lord, Granny inspects everything and then some."

She said, "Draw him some cool water from the well, Danny." I was exhausted so I decided to do it my way. After all, the well water had to be drawn out bucket by bucket, then poured into a larger container. I got the water from the pump on the back porch, threw in a few handfuls of dirt to give it the appearance of coming from a well, stirred it in, and dragged the tin tub over to the mule's trough. He just stood there and refused to drink it.

I heard Granny's alarming voice from afar saying, "Danny, I know, without even asking you, that you didn't follow my directions. The mule refuses to drink water from the pump. That's why I told you to draw the water from the well. By not following my directions, it is as if you gave him no water at all. I'm sure you learned in school that all living things need water to survive. Without water supplied by God, no life form on Earth would exist. I want you to get two small pots and plant three cantaloupe seeds in each one of them. Water only one of the pots and leave the other one completely dry. Check on them daily to see if the water makes a difference. The mule needs his water and we are ready for you to do it right this time."

I did as Granny said and the mule drank the well water as if he could not get enough.

"Danny," said Granny, "I'm like that ol' mule over there when it comes to the Word of God. I want to drink of that living water until I thirst no more." *Oh wow*, I thought, *here we go again*. I thought I had gotten away from the words of that old Miss Bertha Mae Brown. It was like her words followed me all the way down south to my Grandma Bretta Jones's house, who happened to be one of her friends. All I could think was *what a shame and somebody please give me a break*!

I don't know why these old people just wouldn't leave me alone. They've lived their lives, now it was my turn to live mine. I just wanted them to let me be and get out of my face with all of that old-timey stuff. I wasn't going for it. I didn't ask for their advice and I didn't want or need it. Then I turned and looked at Granny. She had a beautiful smile on her face.

She said, "I know that this is all new for you and I forgive you for not getting it right the first time. However, now you have been told what the mule likes and expects when it comes to his water, and I know that you have learned that shortcuts don't always work, but often turn the task into a larger one." Granny went on to state, "He might be a mule, but he is a smart mule, smart enough to know that you were trying to pull a fast one on him. Him not drinking the first water you presented was his way of saying that you need to get it together, kid, and stop trying to insult his intelligence. We all make mistakes. No one is perfect. If there is a positive thing about making a mistake it's to learn from it." Granny's conversation turned to tonight's main event. She spoke excitedly about going to the revival at her church, Beauty Grove Baptist Church, and said that it will be held Monday through Friday starting at 7:00 p.m. because that's when the weather tends to cool down a bit. I was not at all interested in going to a revival; my main concern was for my survival. My plans for a cool refreshing shower, putting on my favorite PJs, and going to bed early were completely leveled. I did get to take a shower and put on some clean clothes, but then we were off to the revival.

I was super tired after working on Granny's small farm that day. As soon as the revival service was over for the night, I got in her car and slept all the way back to the house. When we got home, I went directly to what used to be my father's old bedroom when he was a child, with the thought of getting prepared for bed. The next thing I knew, it was Tuesday morning and I woke up fully clothed, with my socks and shoes still on.

CHAPTER FOUR

THE GREAT AGENDA

Tuesday

When I woke up that morning, the smell of hotcakes, scrambled eggs, and sausage links drew me straight to the kitchen. Granny and I exchanged morning greetings. I sat down ready to eat when Granny said, "Just a minute, Danny, before you begin to eat, I need you to first go back and brush your pearly whites and wash your face and hands. Don't take too long because your food will get cold. You can take your shower after we have breakfast."

When I returned to the table, she said grace and we began to eat. I don't know why everything she cooks is so delicious. She is a super cook with a special touch. I don't have to pick up a salt or pepper shaker for anything. She knows how to season the food exactly right. We finished eating and she said that she would clear the table and for me to go take my shower and to get ready for a productive day.

I returned to the kitchen and received my agenda for the day starting with "Your first chore is to go back to your room, make up your bed, and pick up the clothes you threw on the floor. I am the head cook; therefore, that makes you the head dishwasher. No spots are permitted to be left on my plates, glasses, pots, or pans."

Granny went on to say, "Spotless dishes kind of imitate life. For example, if I held up a large white sheet with a black spot on it about the size of a dime and asked you to describe what you saw, like most people, you would probably concentrate on that black spot, regardless of the rest of the sheet that is in mint condition. So often this way of thinking unfortunately imitates life. Some people find it hard to remember the good someone has done once they have learned of a blemish on their character. Let's face it. Some people lie, cheat, steal, or do other undesirable things. For example, once a person has developed the reputation of being a thief, guilty or not, he moves to the top of the list of suspects when something goes missing. This is why it is so important to keep your life as spot free as possible. If you went to a restaurant and were given silverware with dried-up food on it, you probably wouldn't accept it and would rightfully request a clean set. So, if possible, no spots please. The Bible says that Jesus is coming back looking for a church that is without spot or wrinkle. Sweep the kitchen floor, then use your decision-making skills to determine if it needs to be mopped based on your observation."

Granny continued, "You learned yesterday about the care of the animals. They need to be fed every day just like most of us. The mule has eaten all of his hay, so go to the barn and throw down another bale from the loft. I've already fed the dog so put the scraps left from breakfast in the slop bucket for the hogs. We are thankful for all that God has provided; therefore, we don't want to be wasteful. When you go outside, I want you to catch the fattest hen in the yard. Put that washtub from the back porch over it and give it some cracked corn and fresh water daily."

I listened and did what Granny said, but thought, *how weird?* She continued to state that using the washtub was a purification method that she used to produce excellent flavor in her chickens by controlling their diet, unlike free-range, chickens who eat anything. Grandma finished by saying that she believes what they say about us being what we eat. She gave an example about a child she knew who had eaten an abundance of fresh carrots daily and ended up with tinted bright orange-colored palms. The coloration did not revert until carrots were restricted from his diet.

I went back to my dad's old bedroom to pick my clothes up from the floor, which was just the beginning of another chore-filled day. I had to take care of the animals and I dreaded having to catch and contain a live chicken. Yikes! Just thinking about it gave me the heebie-jeebies. The more I thought about it, the more agitated I became. I started mumbling to myself about my dissatisfaction at having to be here and do so much hard work around the farm. Then forcefully, in one swipe, I knocked everything off the top of the dresser to the floor. I spewed out hatred about everybody and everything that stood in my way, including that old Miss Bertha Mae Brown. Unfortunately, I was louder than I thought. Granny heard every word I said and was immediately standing in the doorway with her feet firmly planted on the floor and her hands propped up on her hips, ready to totally blast me.

She gave me a look I shall never forget. It was a look of "Boy, you really just messed up big time." She said, "No one is allowed to disrespect me or my house. Evidently, you don't know who you are dealing with, boy! Your dad was not allowed to be disrespectful to me or any other adult, and neither are you. Disrespect gets you nowhere, but it displays to others the state of your heart, your mind, and your soul." Granny said that she had been observing me and that she could see that I was troubled. She asked if there was something wrong with my heart.

I quickly told her that I had passed my physical examination in order to play football.

She said, "No, Danny, I'm not referring to the muscle pumping in your chest. It appears to me that you may have developed a condition known as a 'stone heart.'" She looked directly in my eyes and said, "I can see and feel your pain. Take off your fake mask—you're not fooling anybody—and get real with yourself and real with your God. I'm your grandma, baby, I love you and I always will. Agape love, which is the highest form of love, needs to be interwoven into the fabric of your life."

I took Granny's advice, the best advice I ever received. Talking to God helped me to realize that when everyone around me falls short of my expectations, it's time to take a good look at myself. Imperfection is a part of life. No one is perfect!

Wednesday

I got up early because, at my Granny's house, there is no such thing as lounging around when there is work to be done. I brushed my teeth, washed my face and hands, then went directly to the kitchen. Today was oatmeal day. We added brown sugar, homemade butter, huckleberries, strawberries, and walnuts. It tasted like a dessert for breakfast. It was so good that I ate two full large bowls, happily cleared the table, washed the dishes, and swept the kitchen floor. I tidied up my room and set out to do my chores. Before going outside, however, I had to mentally prepare myself for a face-off with a mean rooster who had been on my case ever since I arrived.

Every time I went outside, a mean ol' rooster would charge towards me, all puffed up, trying to pick a fight. I've learned that this type of rooster is called a red cap because of the large bright rose-colored comb on the top of its head; therefore, the name "Redcap" seemed fitting for him. I've learned three things about him since my arrival. First, he is going to crow too early in the morning, signaling that it's time to get up; second, he's armed with natural weapons, a sharp beak and long sharp nails; and third, without a doubt, he'll try to pick a fight with me. The other chickens don't do that, it's just him. Is his behavior nature or nurture? I think it's the result of nature because he doesn't show any signs of having been nurtured. I also think when it comes to a real fight, he is definitely what my friends back home would call a yellow belly chicken.

A few weeks back, Granny called my dad and told him about how a little red hen had gone on a stroll with her newly hatched chicks. There, siting high on a tree branch and peering down at the happy-go-lucky family, was a renowned predator: a chicken hawk. The sight of it spelled danger with a capital "D." It was ready for a meal and swooped down to take what it wanted. The little red hen did her best to protect her little chicks. She spread her wings as they ran underneath them. When the chicken hawk swooped down to take, destroy, and devour one of them, she was outmatched like a heavyweight boxer challenging a ten-year-old kid. Although she was outmatched, she put up a heroic fight and fought till her death. So, my question is, why does that same high-strutting, ready-to-attack-me rooster, who was nowhere to be found during the hawk's confrontation with the hen, always want to challenge me? What's up with that? He's just a big bowl of chicken salad. As far as I was concerned, its bullying days were over, as of that day. I clapped my hands and stomped my feet as loud as I could. The sound startled him and he ran away. Later that day, I got the cracked corn and fresh water ready for the fatty hen. I looked around and there stood the red cap rooster, raising up and itching for a fight. I wanted to throw something at him, but there was nothing on the ground near me. I had a little extra cracked corn in my pocket and I threw it in his direction. He ate it and searched the immediate area for more. On that day, I accidently made a new barnyard friend.

The days continued to come and to go. The longer I stayed, the more I learned about what Granny expected of me. I even started to look forward to going to the revival after a hard day of work on the small farm. All of the girls were checking me out. It made me feel kind of good. The preacher's daughter even winked at me, not once but twice. I just played it cool and flashed her a smile. There were some fine sistas in that church. I was excited about going back that night to check out some more girls; that is, if I had the strength to attend. I loved my Granny, but she was a tough taskmaster. All I could say is "Go Granny, go Granny, go!"

Jamming at the Church

The guitar player from the Dew Drop Inn Club was invited to play with the piano player down at the church, along with a drummer. They were once members of that church, but had strayed. One musician from a neighboring church called The House of God, a holiness church, played the steel guitar. It sounded like he could make the instrument talk. Man, those dudes could really play. They had it going on up there. People came early to be sure to get a seat. Those who arrived late walked briskly, almost running through the doorway, eager to get their praise on. I just relaxed, watched, and took it all in.

As I watched the others doing their thing, a set of eyes was being lasered on me. There I go again, thinking about that old Miss Bertha Mae Brown saying that you never know who is watching you. After the service, my admirer, who wore a short, sleeveless red dress and looked about eighteen, five feet four, made a beeline to where I was sitting, welcoming me to the church and introducing herself.

She said, "Hi, my name is Pinky, what's yours?" I told her that my name was Danny Jones, as I got a whiff of her perfume, and that I was in town to visit my grandmother, Mrs. Bretta Jones. She then replied, "Oh yes, I know your grandmother. You must be Daniel and Olivia's son." She then left as quickly as she had appeared, heading towards the vestibule. When I made my way after her, the vestibule was so crowded I could not find that cute chick anywhere. All I knew is that she looked good, smelled good, and that her name was Pinky.

On our way home, I inquired about the lovely Ms. Pinky, which I soon regretted. Grandma put on her stern face and said, "I saw her looking at you up and down at the church. You are a big boy for your age, Danny. She must have thought that she was flirting with someone much older than the same age of her oldest child. We won't hold that against her because she probably wasn't aware of your youthful age. I want you to know that men are naturally drawn to her and when she comes around, many ladies cling tighter to their significant others. But my advice to you on how to handle this delicate situation is to speak kindly, but keep it moving for you are not Pinky's equal. She looks young, but she is a full-fledged grown woman. I know people can change and that God forgives, but for now, since I am responsible for your well-being, I'm telling you, she is out of your range. Please do not get caught up in her alluring spell. I need you to be obedient and not cause your heart to be troubled, for Pinky Dupree is too much of a woman for a young person like you."

CHAPTER FIVE

GRANNY THE CHEMIST?

Wednesday was a very eventful day. In addition to doing my regular chores, I was delighted to learn that Granny was known, in this area, for being somewhat of a natural chemist. People would often come to her for a rubbing ointment that would speed up the healing process of scrapes and bruises. Dr. Copeland would send his nurse to Granny's house to get small containers of it for his patients. Some said that it even helped to regrow hair. Unfortunately, while I did not learn the formula, I could smell that sulfur was definitely one of its main ingredients. She would go to a wooded area on her property and harvest bark from certain types of trees, along with a variety of herbs. She boiled her gatherings together and added other natural ingredients to the batch. Granny had remedies for just about anything that ailed you. She even had remedies for bladder infections, coughs, and many other ailments. She'd also delivered a few babies when the doctor hadn't arrived in time. The knowledge of our ancestors passed down from generation to generation continues to serve us well. The window washing solution she made has kept her windows sparkling clean and my sinuses cleared. When I first arrived, Granny noticed that I had some issues with my sinus cavities. Unbeknownst to me at the time, she added a compound to the window cleaning solution to help ease my discomfort and I'm glad she did. I have not had a sinus headache since I washed her windows. I now understand why my dad would jokingly tease her about practicing medicine without a license. But one thing was for sure, she found many cures by making homemade remedies: one in particular included corn silk, something that many of us take for granted and throw away.

One day a man came by the house from a neighboring county. He said that he had heard, over the years, so many good things about Granny that he wanted to have the pleasure of meeting her. He wandered around a bit and started asking questions about some of her homemade remedies. They continued to talk for about forty-five minutes, with obvious long pauses during the conversation.

She then asked him point-blank, "Why are you really here and is there a specific type of remedy you are seeking?" He lowered his voice to just above a whisper, which caused my ears to perk up even more to hear what he was saying. He told her that he has a daughter who had come home from college "in trouble" and inquired if she had something, or could make up a remedy, to help her get out of the situation? I didn't know exactly what he meant, but Granny certainly did. She had the look of being both insulted and disgusted simultaneously. Without batting an eye, she told him that she worked for the

Lord and not the devil. She picked up her homemade straw broom and began to sweep sand off the porch. She swept from one end to the other, then went over to the area where the man was still sitting and made gestures that he needed to get up and move so she could complete the job. When he angrily and aggressively stood up and kicked the chair he'd been sitting in, I stood up too, to send that man a silent but clear message that he was out of line and that I was there to look out for my Granny's well-being.

Without a word, he began to hastily leave; however, Granny had a few parting words of wisdom for him, saying, "You never know who will give you your last glass of water, sir. Take good care of your daughter and love the future within her with all of your heart, mind, and soul and everything will be alright." The man began to slowly nod his head, signaling that he understood the coded message and he apologized and begged for her forgiveness.

It was almost time for our usual trek down to the church. We had just had a quick afternoon shower and Granny decided she wanted to go and take a look at her vegetable garden. When we walked over to it, she pulled three string beans from a plant, broke off the tips, and ate the long slender beans raw. She walked down to the okra plants and ate a couple of okra pods too. Granny told me that okra was her favorite vegetable. She liked them fried, stewed, and even raw. Sometimes she said she would place a few of them in a pot on top of cooked butterbeans and peas, then steam them gently until they were tender. She called that "good eating." She relayed to me that okra seeds were probably brought over from Africa to America by slaves who were captured as they had been working in the fields planting okra and still had some of the seeds left in their pockets. I was impressed by this information, but my taste buds and Granny's taste buds are as far apart as the East Coast is from the West Coast when it comes to being a fan of okra. I started to choose a string bean too but decided a small, fresh pickling-sized cucumber would probably be more appealing to my palate. I later decided against it and instead chose a large, bright red, juicy, vine-ripened beefsteak tomato that still had raindrops clinging to it. I hit the jackpot. It was delicious, the best tomato I'd ever put in my mouth. I'd heard how important it is to eat fresh fruit and vegetables brought directly from the farm to the table, but that day I experienced an even better treat. The tomato I ate came from a plant in Granny's garden, then went directly into my mouth! You can't get anything fresher than that and it was inconceivably good.

We went to church and everything unfolded practically in the same manner as the previous nights. But what caught my attention was Rev. Joyner's sermon, when he emphasized that the devil is a strong opponent with a humongous following. He shared that the devil is a super tough adversary and he is ready to help defeat him as souls are saved for Jesus Christ. He was really sincere about doing the work of the Lord. Rev. Joyner repeatedly stated that if we chose not to acknowledge God in this world then when it comes time to determine where we will dwell for infinity, it will not be with Him. He told the congregation that if they didn't want to take his word for it, he encouraged them to turn their Bibles to Matthew 10:33 which states, "But whosoever shall deny me before men, him will I also deny before my Father which is in heaven." As Rev. Joyner preached, I pondered to myself, "Would God really do that to us?" That is, cast us off to the depths of hell? According to the Bible, the answer is a resounding "Yes."

Church dismissed and we walked out to the vestibule. There, in a circle of five, stood two teenage boys, who appeared to be a little older than me, and two elderly men, who happened to be deacons of the church, along with Pinky, who served as the anchor of the group and held their undivided attention. Pinky had flirted with me last evening; was she also flirting with them? Oh my, how I wished I could be a part of that circle. I heard one of the older men say to her, "Ms. Pinky, I see you still have those lovely little pink lips just like your mama." I thought to myself, lips my foot, just who does he think he's fooling with his eyes focused well below Pinky's neck. The mammary glands we learned about in our Life Science class back in middle school were definitely on display. They were there for any and everybody who might be interested in taking a good look. I could not believe it; I had a tough time wrapping my head around it. Were my eyes deceiving me? As I looked at the circle of men staring at Pinky's scantily covered chest, Granny came over and put one of her arms firmly around my shoulder and calmly, without saying a word, led me straight out the front door of the church and directly to her car.

I remember when I was in middle school, my Life Science teacher gave us a list of vocabulary words to learn and to use in complete sentences. I had to do the same for my Language Arts class. This concept of team teaching across the curriculum was beginning to pay off big-time. I could now use the word "voluptuous" learned from my Language Arts class list along with "mammary glands" learned from my Life Science list in complete sentences without any hesitation. The lessons taught in those classes were beginning to make more sense to me. I wish I had been more in tune and paid closer attention in my classes. I could feel a light summer breeze as Granny and I walked towards her car. That kind, gentle, sweet grandma who had met me at the closed gas station a few days earlier with wide-open arms was now on a strategic mission.

She began the conversation by saying, "Baby, I know you want to find your place in this world, but I feel that I must make you aware of some obvious pitfalls in life you may have not even considered. You really need to have a talk with your dad, but since you are here with me and in my care, I must use this time as a teachable moment. There are a lot of nice young and respectable girls in this world; however, I noticed Pinky was the one who caught your eye and figuratively put a large hook up your nose. I can't tell you who to like, date, or eventually one day, who to marry. I want you to take time to read in your Bible about different types of women. Be sure to include the folly women and read about the virtuous woman (Proverbs 9:13-18; Proverbs 31:10-31). I want you to be fully prepared to ward off unnecessary drama in your life. When someone shows an interest in you, and you think that you might have an interest in them, check them out thoroughly. Even some of the most beautiful and fragrant flowers can have bees hidden in them. You've got to remember to look before you smell the roses. If not, you may get unexpectedly stung."

Granny continued, "In the Bible there is a story about a couple known as Samson and Delilah. Samson was an extraordinarily strong man. Delilah persuaded him to divulge the secret of his strength. He did and she used it against him. Remember, everybody does not always have your best interest at heart. I'm here to tell you that the same kind of people on Earth during the biblical days still exist today. You need to be aware of what God says about different situations when making a decision. After all, everything that glitters is not gold. For example, sometimes things are exactly the opposite of how they appear. Does salt not look like sugar? Yes, it does, but try baking a cake using salt in place of the sugar. It can be done, but the question is, is that what you really want? There are some things in life we need to repel for our own good. In the Bible for example, Joseph ran from Potiphar's wife, who wanted him to sin. He knew that he had to get away from her and ran out of his cloak. When I was a teenager, a musical group called Smokey Robinson and the Miracles recorded a song with advice a caring mother gave to her young son. It warned that 'You Better Shop Around' before making a decision that could affect you for the rest of your life. You are at a stage in your life whereby you are not a little child anymore, but are definitely not yet a man. I call this as being on the cusp of change. You have to crawl before you walk and walk before you run. Therefore, you must be thoroughly prepared before you set out to win a marathon. When you become a man, build your house on a solid foundation: a home that is full of love, happiness, and respect."

When we arrived back at Granny's house, I was obedient and I read in my Bible about some of the women, but the thought of the lovely Ms. Pinky Dupree continued to weigh heavily on my mind. I tried to shake it off but I just couldn't stop thinking about her. I wondered if this was love or what they call infatuation, or maybe something else I'd been hearing a lot about lately—hormones. Could it be that? Whatever it was, I could still recall the fresh fragrance she left when she walked past my pew. The fragrance was like the white gardenia flowers my dad gave to my mom last Valentine's Day. I went to bed, but all I could do was softly say her name as I drifted off to sleep: Pinky, Pinky, Pinky. The thought of her beauty and pleasantries followed me into the dream world. I had a dream of being at a formal dinner. Pinky was also invited. We sat and ate at a huge table. The host showered us with kindness. He displayed a gentleness about himself that was very appealing. Towards the conclusion of the dinner, the host poured the remaining punch that was left in the punch bowl into one cup to make what he called a "love cup." He gave a toast, took a sip from the "love cup," then passed it to the dinner guest to his right. We were encouraged to give a toast, take a sip from the cup, and pass it to the next guest. The ritual continued and the cup was finally passed to me. I was the last guest to receive it because I sat to the immediate left of the host. I said the traditional toast, then placed the "love cup" on the table without indulging. In my dream, when I received the "love cup" and said a toast, but did not sip from the cup, questions were launched at me, asking why did I not sip from the cup? My answer was too many lips had supped from that cup;

therefore, I chose not to sip. I dreamed that same dream several times that night and woke up tired, awash in a cold sweat, and almost in a panic attack. My body felt like I had been in a wrestling match all night long.

The next morning, I felt extremely weak and could not get that dream out of my head. I wished I knew a dream interpreter to get the meaning of it. I talked with Granny about it and she suggested that I call my dad to see if he could shed any light on it. He said that he really didn't know but perhaps my subconscious was trying to solve a concern that was weighing heavily on me. My dad prayed with me over the phone and asked God to give me peace of mind. After we prayed, I felt like a burden had been lifted from my shoulders and I started to feel like my old self again. Thank you, Jesus.

CHAPTER SIX

PREPARING TO VISIT
THE SICK AND SHUT-IN

Thursday

Thursday morning, I slept a little later than usual. When I awoke, I didn't detect anything being cooked in the kitchen. It was unusual for Granny not to have a good breakfast prepared and it was already a little past time for us to eat.

I went to the kitchen and she said, "I need you to help carry this pot of hot water out to the back porch." She had in her hand two pot holders that one of her friend's children had made for her as a birthday present. She passed one over to me to use on one of the hot handles on the large pot. She caught hold of one handle and I the other as we walked slowly, with precision, to avoid any spillage. She then said, "Thank you very much, Danny, now please go back inside and make yourself some breakfast, then take time to let your food digest for about twenty minutes or so before you return. By then, I'll be ready for your help."

I went back in the house, made and ate two peanut butter sandwiches, one with muscadine grape jam and the other with honey, along with a plump banana. I didn't feel quite full so I scrambled three eggs, added some shredded cheese on top, and ate them too. The breakfast was finished off with a large glass of cold, un-pasteurized, sweet milk Granny had gotten from one of her neighbors. It was very rich; cream was visible on top of the milk in my glass. It was a surprisingly good breakfast. Now it was time to relax and to let my digestion system—one of the eleven major organ systems in the body—do its thing. I was beginning to realize that I learned more than I thought in my classes and would have learned even more if I had paid closer attention.

The proper amount of time passed and I was ready to go back outside to help Granny. Lordy, Lordy, what a shocker. When I saw what she was doing, I jumped clean off the porch. The fatty hen I had placed under the wash-tub, fed cracked corn, and provided with fresh water daily was about to go with us to visit the sick and shut-in. Feathers were flying everywhere as Granny prepared it to be the main ingredient in her chicken, vegetable, and wide noodle soup. The feathers continued to come off as the hen was repeatedly dipped in and out of the big pot of hot water to loosen the grip on the feathers. The hen now looked like the ones we buy from the grocery store back home except that this fowl's skin was as yellow as a beautiful bright sunflower. I learned from my mom that a chicken with deep yellow skin is very tasty because it has been fed a good diet.

Granny smiled and said, "I'm proud of you, Danny, you did a great job tending to this chicken. Your work will be appreciated by the sick and shut-in more than you will ever know. Thank you."

In addition to my role as head dishwasher, I also held the position of assistant cook. My major responsibility was to prep the vegetables for the soup. I was directed to use all of the white potatoes left in the potato bin because it was time for the deacons to visit the widowers of the church and they would replenish it. I washed the small white potatoes and scraped the skin off with a butter knife. I did the carrots the same way and chopped them into bite-size pieces. Next, I shelled a half peck of sweet peas that Granny had picked from her garden. The hulls were still damp from the morning dew. The peas had a beautiful green hue about them, not dulled like the ones we buy back home in a can.

Granny is fantastic. She is direct and very confident and I like those character traits about her. You don't have to spend time guessing what she expects from you. She believes in doing things right the first time, if possible. Granny said that she would prefer to make an entire dress correctly from the beginning to the end instead of having to make alterations. That might be the reason she cooked that chicken, vegetable, and wide noodle soup for such a long time.

She cooked it low and slow for most of the morning so the flavors could come together gently to complement each other. Once the soup has cooked, she does not add anything else to it because she knows it is just right.

Last night after returning home from church, Granny baked four loaves of Ezekiel (which means "God strengthens") bread. She said that the recipe has been around for thousands of years. She keeps large jars of the ingredients in her food pantry at all times so that she is always prepared to make what some people call Bible bread, while others call it manna bread. The ingredients for this bread can actually be found in the Bible beginning at Ezekiel 4:9.

Granny began to chuckle to herself and then said, "Yes, I use all of the listed ingredients for the bread; however, I don't use the recommended fuel for baking it. I just use my regular old dependable oven for my baking." I looked at Granny, waiting for her to tell me about the fuel recommended in the Bible. She said, "I bet you are waiting for me to tell you about the fuel. Well, I'm not going to tell you because you might think it's something I just made up. Besides, I've already told you where you can begin your research. You can't expect others to do things for you that you are capable of doing for yourself. I'm sure you have heard the saying that God helps those who help themselves. If you really want the answer to the type of mystery fuel, seek and ye shall find. When the answer is revealed to you, I want you to keep in mind that this bread could still be baked with that same type of fuel, but during our lifetime, God has showered us with so many wonderful blessings through the knowledge he has bestowed upon mankind, so I prefer to use the new type of fuel. The information in the Bible holds the key to us having a more abundant life, from birth to eternity. The Bible is the most powerful book ever written. No other literature can compete or uproot it because it stands on the solid word of God. God is the Word!"

Since I got here, peacefulness was beginning to become a part of my life. I'd taken the time to look around and to appreciate the beauty of such things as a variety of colorful wildflowers, picking and eating scattered huckleberries, the fresh smell of the earth immediately after a quick summer shower, the cool breeze and shade from the trees, the fishing hole filled with an abundance of freshwater fish, beautiful green leafy vegetables, and that magnificent woman I'm blessed to have as my grandmother.

I used to think of Granny as being somewhat like Miss Bertha Mae Brown—old-fashioned, obsolete, and out of the loop, not hip when it came to using technology. Granny still used a landline phone with a rotary dial. She knew business telephone numbers, as well as the numbers of her family and friends, without any hesitation, completely from memory. One day, after calling my parents, I misplaced my cell phone. I felt like I was up a creek without a paddle. I looked and looked for it.

Granny said, "Danny, use my landline phone and call your cell number to see if you can hear it ring." She was standing in the kitchen as I nervously tried to call it six or seven times, getting a wrong number each time. I'd just gotten a phone a couple days before my phone privileges were revoked and didn't have the chance to commit my new number to memory.

I said, "I can't get through, I don't remember any of the numbers programmed in my cell." The only number I remembered was 911, but even knowing 911 couldn't help me out in this situation.

She said, "Call the following number." I did and the sound of a ringing phone came from my back pocket. She asked me to pass the landline phone over to her and directed me to answer the one ringing in my pocket. I said hello, and of course it was Granny on the other line saying, "A word to the wise, let your brain do its job, use it. Learn your cell phone number, please. I know it and it isn't even mine. Sear that number into your brain. One day, it could make a difference in your life or the lives of others." I took the time that very same day and learned my number. I was determined to learn it because I did not want Granny to catch me off guard again without memorizing that number.

Pen and Paper

Granny did not do a lot of talking on her phone; however, when she used it, she would have a notebook and a pen at her fingertips in case she had to write anything down. That way, she wouldn't have to tell someone to hold on while she found a pen or a piece of paper. She was always ready. When she took notes, I became aware that her writing was different and I couldn't decipher anything that she wrote. I wanted to know why it looked so different and if she could understand what it meant. Of course, she could and started to tell me about how women used to be discriminated against in the workplace and in other areas. The mystery marks I was inquiring about were known as shorthand. It was a way of rapidly writing by using symbols to replace the alphabet. A lot of young women who wanted out of domestic or factory work were taught typing and shorthand skills to help them qualify for entry-level work in the clerical field. Those skills would get them in the door, but all too often, they would not advance as quickly as their male counterparts. In many jobs, the men made more money than the ladies doing the same exact work from the start. The excuse the administration used for the discrepancy was that men had to take care of their families. Well, what about the single mother who had the same responsibility as the head of the household? This issue caused "hot beds" of discussion amongst employees and, on some jobs, they were forbidden from discussing salaries. It was made crystal clear that this kind of discussion would be grounds for immediate termination, which put a stop to them requesting equal pay. Every mother knows it's more important to have a pot full of beans for her children to eat than a pot full of nothing.

Granny said, "Sometimes we have to do what we have to do for survival until a new day cometh, and it shall."

Granny said the workplace had gotten somewhat better but there was still a lot to overcome in some places of employment. "Back in the day," said Granny, "if a man was available to be the principal of a school, more than likely he was the principal, and the women, for the most part, were the teachers. Likewise, in the field of medicine, a man was usually the doctor and the women were often the nurses. In addition, men were usually the president or CEO of many companies and organizations and the women were personal assistants or secretaries. While there is nothing wrong with a male or female being a teacher, nurse, or personal assistant, competent, skilled women should not be overlooked for jobs just because of their gender. We have come a long way, but we have a long way to go. Please do not underestimate the power of the woman. Every human being came to Earth by way of a woman, even Jesus Christ. We are thankful for the progress, but will not rest until we get equal pay for equal work." Granny said, "It seems like women are beginning to get more credit nowadays. Work is work and women should receive equal pay for doing the same job as men. I seriously doubt if a man who received less pay than a woman for doing the same work would stand for it! It's just not in a man's nature. I like the fact that human beings can think, reason, and do the right thing. But the male species of some animals, like 'Redcap' for example, continue to dominate. I've come to believe that his behavior is not nurture, but a classic example of nature."

Granny continued, "Danny, I've heard too many times about African American men and women being excited about their selection to train new employees, only later to find out that the new white employee they trained has now become their supervisor. Nowadays you need not sit back and wait for others to determine your future. Take hold of your own reins and get involved in shaping your success. You need to get busy in a positive way."

CHAPTER SEVEN

THE PROFESSOR
AND MRS. TAYLOR

The plan for this evening was to visit the sick and shut-in on our way to the revival service. We loaded the car with several containers of the homemade chicken soup and the four loaves of Ezekiel bread, along with a batch of sugar cookies. Granny began to explain how everybody has a story to tell and that some have more struggles to bear than others. She elaborated that her main mission was to help and not to judge, but wanted to share with me some well-known facts about those she thought could benefit from her mission work. We were going to make three stops today. The first visit would be at the home of Elliot and Violet Taylor. Nadine Watson and her children were our second stop and then we were going to visit a man notoriously known throughout the county—Alford Covington.

Granny said that Elliot and Violet Taylor were long-time educators and now a retired couple. They complemented each other like peanut butter and jelly. Mr. Taylor was often referred to as "Professor." He served as the principal of Spring Hope Elementary School for a few decades. Most of the students referred to Mrs. Taylor as their favorite teacher. Mrs. Taylor walked with a cane in her right hand, and Mr. Taylor walked with his cane in his left hand, so that they could continue to hold each other's hand after almost sixty years of marriage. The Taylors were a childless couple and took valuable time with their students to bring out the best in them. They nurtured one particular student who was grossly neglected and in need. That former student, who now referred to them as Ma Taylor and Pa Taylor, lived a few miles down the road from them, with her husband and their children. They referred to her as their precious little angel sent by God. She and her family checked up on the Taylors, either by way of home visits or phone calls, to make sure that they were doing well and had whatever they might need. The Taylors described their faithfulness to them as beyond compare.

The Taylors are very valuable to this community. They are held in high esteem. Granny said, "I'll never forget the day when I looked out of the front room window and saw the Professor's car coming towards the house. I recognized him as the driver. In the back seat, I could see the tip-top of two little children's heads. To my surprise, when the car got closer to the house, I could see that it was your daddy and your Aunt Claire. Your daddy had taken a snapping turtle to school in his book sack. Instead of taking out a book, as instructed by the teacher, he took out a long-necked snapping turtle, which is known for its powerful jaws. He took it to school to chase the girls during recess. Claire saw your daddy being escorted to the Professor's office, so she followed. The Professor said that when he was about to administer the standard corporal punishment of three licks with the paddle, known as 'The Board of Education,' the small finger on his right hand was severely bitten, causing him excruciating pain. He said he had to do a double take to make sure that it was little Claire and not the snapping turtle who had ripped into his skin. Sure enough, it was confirmed that it was the angelic-looking little Claire who had done the damage because the snapping turtle was still in your dad's book sack. The Professor was quite outdone. He said that he'd always heard that a snapping turtle had such strong jaws and that if one bit you, it would not turn you loose until it thundered. Still, he said he wished it were the snapping turtle that had bitten him and not little Claire. While the physical bite hurt, the pain he felt deep down in the depth of his heart at being bitten by little Claire was almost unbearable. Aunt Claire had disappointed him in a way no one could ever understand.

"He said he brought the children home so the school and parents could be on the same page for a corrective plan. While he loved my children dearly, the Professor said it was his responsibility, as principal of Spring Hope Elementary School, to carry out the rules of the school district. He continued. 'My people are destroyed for the lack of knowledge as in Hosea 4:6,' the Professor said in a quivering voice. 'Besides, I refuse to allow my students to become another generation of uneducated cotton pickers. They've got to study hard, have hope, and rise up to become competitive in this world.'"

Granny said, "The Professor requested permission to proceed in carrying out his duty right there in my living room. Your dad received the standard punishment of three licks for not doing his schoolwork and for disturbing the class. You know that when someone disrupts class, other students are robbed of an opportunity to gain knowledge. Knowledge is power. We can't afford to miss out on any of it. Claire, rightfully so, received five firm licks for sticking her nose in where it didn't belong. Legally, this is known as an accessory after the fact. Also, if Claire had been an older child, the Professor could have filed an assault charge against her for the injury he sustained from that bite. It was an ugly bite. I could hardly believe my eyes or my ears; yet, there standing in front of me were my children, my flesh and my blood, guilty as charged. I earnestly begged the Professor's pardon on their behalf. We agreed that this intolerable behavior must be stopped, and stopped now. Then, I told them to ask for forgiveness for being disobedient and disrespectful and they did, though it was barely audible over the sounds of loud snorts and sniffles."

Granny continued, "If Claire were home from Ghana, West Africa, which was once known as the Gold Coast, she would undoubtedly tell you, without hesitation, that she learned a very valuable lesson that day many years ago in the Professor's office. She said Professor Taylor looked directly at her and said, 'If you're grown, stay home,' then loaded them up in his car and brought them straight to me. That day, she learned not to be an agitator, to show respect for those who are in charge, and to mind her own business. Claire said, as a missionary, she often shares with others that infamous day in her life and that Professor Taylor made such an impact on her that it was her first and last day of her getting in trouble at school. She clearly remembers her punishment was far worse than that of her brother's because she injected herself into the situation, causing it to escalate.

"As the Professor was leaving, he turned and said, 'Daniel and Claire, I've been given the challenge of making sure that my people get a good education and I take my responsibility solemnly. Do you understand?' Your dad and aunt replied, 'Yes, sir, Mr. Professor.'

"The Professor responded, saying, 'Answer me in a complete sentence. Yes, sir, Mr. Professor, WHAT?'

"They replied, 'Yes, sir, Mr. Professor, we understand.'"

Now I understood why my dad was such a stickler about Lil' Sis and me answering him in complete sentences.

Granny said, "Needless to say, when the Professor left my house and returned to school with the back seat of his car empty, it sent a loud and clear message to my children and me that this type of behavior would not be tolerated from them or anyone else. That was Phase I. Phase II was yet to come, which was, 'Wait 'til your father gets home.'"

Granny said, "Claire and her family visit the Professor and Mrs. Taylor just about every time they return home from Ghana. Even though the Professor has had Alzheimer's for a few years now, the running joke when she visits is 'Bretta, is that little Claire with you, or is it that mean ol' snapping turtle?' I assure him that it's Claire and not the turtle. Then he adds, 'My sight isn't as good as it used to be, I just wanted to be sure before I asked

Violet to get prepared to cook up some good old stewed turtle and rice.' Then he laughs so hard until he goes into a belly roll and enjoys every second of it. Then he calms down and says to Claire, 'Come here, my little Claire, and let me have the honor of hugging your neck. I'm so proud of you and your husband, Kofi, for being missionaries in Ghana, and your brother Daniel being a zoologist up north in that large laboratory. He's doing an excellent job trying to save the animals created by God.' He also asks about your mother, wanting to know if she is still keeping those doctors up there straight. He also insists to Mrs. Taylor that if he ever needs surgery, he's going to have it done up there at that big hospital where your mother works. He has always had a lot of confidence in her and only wants Olivia to be his nurse anesthetist. Mrs. Taylor sweetly replies, 'Yes, dear, yes, dear.'"

When we arrived at the Taylors' residence, I was told to knock on the door and to give them some extra time to answer it. Granny explained that the Taylors had slowed down quite a bit during the last year or two. When the door opened, there stood Mrs. Taylor, with her stylish cane, warmly welcoming us into her home. She looked at me and said, "My, my, Danny, you certainly have grown since I last laid eyes on you. The older you get, the more you look like Daniel."

As soon as I set the soup and Ezekiel bread on the table, the Professor began to tell me a story about how, one day at Spring Hope Elementary School, he challenged the entire school to find the answer to a difficult mathematical word problem. He said, "Olivia was in the third grade, and was the only student to come up with the correct answer. I knew right then and there that she was a 'math whiz.' One day the children at school watched two baby birds leave their nest and do so successfully. There was a third one, however, that was not yet strong enough to fly away and landed hard on the ground and broke one of its legs. Olivia sprang into action, made a splint for the bird's broken leg, and nursed it back to health."

Mrs. Taylor said, "That's right, Danny. At that time Olivia was one of my students and when the bird became strong and healthy, the entire student body went outside to watch as she released it back into its natural environment. I remember Oliva saying, just like it was yesterday, 'Fly, little birdie, fly. Flap your wings and fly high towards the sky.'"

Before Granny and I left the Taylors, Mrs. Taylor asked us to please come back and visit before I returned to Philadelphia. She said she wanted to make something special for me, which she called "a taste of the South." It was fried squash. I almost choked. The only vegetable I dislike more than okra is disgusting squash. We visited the Taylors for approximately twenty minutes and, during our short stay, the Professor asked me at least four times to tell him my name. I did, but I found it to be a little irritating and I tried really hard not to show my true feelings on my face.

When we got back in the car, Granny explained how important it is to have patience with everybody, especially the elderly. "As time passes on, some people develop a condition known as Alzheimer's disease," said Granny. "Alzheimer's is what they used to call dementia when I was a child. During that time, people didn't think too much of it. They would kind of joke about it and move on. You could often hear someone say, for example, 'Don't pay Grandpa any attention, he just has a little touch of dementia.'" I learned from Granny that some people who suffer from Alzheimer's disease don't have a problem remembering the past, like the stories the Professor told me about my mom when she was a kid in the third grade, but find recalling the present, like remembering my name, somewhat challenging.

Granny said, "The Professor continues to make everybody feel good and supported. He continuously makes Claire feel loved and forgiven. Even though many years have passed since the incident, and often he can't remember whether or not he has eaten a meal, that notorious day remains fresh in his mind. That's a good example of being forgiven but not forgotten."

CHAPTER EIGHT

NADINE WATSON

Our next stop was to Nadine Watson's house. On the ten-minute drive, Granny shared several stories about Ms. Nadine and her family. Granny said that she is a good person with a lot of children. She has so many children that some people refer to her like the nursery rhyme: "There was an old woman who lived in a shoe." She is not old, but she has a tremendous responsibility. Granny said, "If I didn't know better, I would think that Nadine was operating a day care center that was full to capacity. Not only does she have all of her children, she also took in some of her relatives' children who had gone up north to find work. She treats them all the same. If you didn't know better, you would not know who she birthed from those who were left in her loving care. She showers them with a tremendous amount of love; some might say tons of love. She is an only child and so is her husband and they prayed to God to bless them with a large family."

Granny said, "When people teased her about having so many children, she would reply, 'God knows best, talk to him.' After all, she would say, 'Look at my darling little children. One day they will do great things.' Quite often, the relatives up north would send lots of clothing for them. The children would become a little giddy when the mailman came to their house to deliver a package that was too large to fit into their mailbox. They would gather around the cardboard box, waiting for it to be opened to see what was in it for them."

Granny said that she always looked forward to this visit because she could feel happiness in the air. She started visiting Ms. Nadine and her children just before she gave birth to the child called "Knee Baby." Granny explained that knee baby is the term given to the child who used to be the youngest of the family, until the arrival of a new baby. Granny said, "How the term knee baby got started, I don't know, but if I had to take a guess at it, I would be inclined to say that, technically, the knee baby is still in need of the mother's attention, often having to relinquish a great deal of it when a new baby arrives. The knees are the closest things to a mother's lap, a place where the baby feels warm and secure; therefore, many times, that's where you will find the knee baby, perhaps waiting for an opportunity to again feel the closeness of his mother's love."

Granny said, "Nadine's family is perhaps what some would consider poor, but I do not agree. The children seem to get excited and grateful for just about anything. I love the way they live. I look forward to seeing them and they look forward to seeing me too. Every week, I can expect something different."

The Chinaberry Tree

Granny said, "Ms. Nadine's children loved to gather under the chinaberry tree in their front yard. This is where they would sing, recite poems, dance, and play games. They played hopscotch, jack rocks, jump rope, and pick up the sticks. They also made mud pies and loved to shoot marbles. Their favorite game was dodge ball, at least until the older boys joined in, since they often deliberately threw the ball too hard. This action always signaled game over. The children loved to shoot firecrackers and would start as early as 6:00 a.m. They loved to sing little jingles that have been passed down for many years such as 'Little Sally Walker Sitting in a Saucer' and 'Here Comes the Lady from Baltimore.' One day, I looked up and saw some of the children coming from across the field, each with a long string of freshwater perch and smiling from ear to ear. One of them said, 'Ms. Bretta, we knew you were coming today, so we caught some extra fish for you. Pick out the ones you want and we will clean them. We don't want you to hurt your hands.' Oh, how thankful and joyous I felt at their good will. Joy ran deep down in my soul."

According to Granny, the children would play all day or were busy doing something. There was a lot of laughter in that house; however, a couple of years earlier, the boys and their visiting friends were playing like they were in the Wild West. The boys would try to see who could start a campfire first by rubbing two sticks together. That's a contest no one won. They played mostly with short sticks to depict weapons and longer ones to represent their horses. They would gallop around in the yard on their pretend horses saying, 'giddyup, horse, giddyup.' One day, one of the neighboring friends came over and showed them his shiny new cap gun. One of the boys got what he thought was a good idea. He ran in the house and retrieved the handgun his father hid in the wardrobe for his family's protection while he was away on duty. Nadine's son and his friend argued about who would get shot first. Her son gave in and agreed to let his friend be first. Tragically, it was all over for his friend and I'm sure signaled a lifetime of sorrow for Nadine's son. They were both only five years old and had played together every day. They were the best of friends who did not understand the real-life consequences of playing with a real gun. They called the police and the little boy's mother interceded, saying to them, "He's just a child, let him go." A few days passed and Ms. Nadine and her family had to face another heartbreaking tragedy. She had placed her toddler out in the front yard, in her stroller, to take in some fresh air and a little sunshine. When Ms. Nadine returned to check on her baby, she saw the mother of the little boy who was tragically shot and killed at her house a few days earlier, walking away from her child. The toddler was still in her stroller chewing on something given to her by the woman and, within seconds, she slumped over and died. That was the last time she saw that neighbor. That woman and her entire family packed up and moved away during the middle of the night, never to be seen or heard from again.

I said, "Oh, Granny, that was so cruel. My parents always tell Lil' Sis and me that 'two wrongs never make a right.'"

Granny continued. "The senseless death of the two children caused Nadine to feel broken and full of agony. She sobbed, prayed, and fasted for many days and asked God to please help her. She prayed to Him for guidance. Her newfound burdens were just too much for her to handle on her own. She prayed to Him to help her not be bitter because she knew she had an enormous responsibility ahead of her, which was to help her children to cope with the tragedies and other deprivations they might encounter in life. Nadine knew that the little boy's death was beyond a terrible tragic accident, but what his mother did to destroy her baby was a malicious act of revenge. She intentionally caused the death of an innocent little child. Granny said that woman must have believed the eye for an eye and a tooth for a tooth doctrine instead of having the spirit of love and forgiveness in her heart. The act intentionally done to that innocent little baby remained with the family and the community for a long time."

Granny said, "I've known Nadine all of her life, but I really didn't get to know her well until I started visiting her and her family, on a regular basis, almost three years ago when she unexpectedly fell seriously ill. She had to be placed on complete bed rest. The naysayers of the community began to wag their sharp barbed wire tongues, trying to attach themselves to anybody who would listen. It was like a frenzy or a race towards who could make up the biggest untruth and tell the most people. I deliberately used the adjective 'barbed wire' because the rumors were vicious, designed to hurt and to destroy. They were so horrible that I didn't repeat them then and definitely won't now. She and her children did not need such nonsense in their lives. What they needed was someone to lend them a helping hand. So, the missionary group I'm a member of volunteered to be her nursemaid. Some of the members cooked food, others washed clothes, cleaned up the house, helped the children with homework, and did whatever else we saw that needed to be done. In a few weeks, the rumors hit a high pitch. No matter where you went, Nadine was the hot topic of the day and for many days to come. Surprisingly, a lot of men also engaged in the rumor mill, too.

"The person who seemed to have the most to say about Nadine's 'alleged' illness was a woman who, in her younger days, thought she would marry Jack Watson, Nadine's husband. Instead, he asked Nadine to be his bride and joined the army to secure their future. The rumors became so bad, until there were some people who didn't even want to be near those of us who had gone to the family's rescue, saying that we might have contracted the same devastating contagious disease. At the peak of the mayhem, Nadine made what some might call a miraculous recovery.

"Guess what name was finally given to the so-called dreadful, sinful, and potentially lethal disease that could possibly spread and wipe out the entire county? The name was Esau Watson, the one we now call Knee Baby!" Nadine was expecting a new addition to her family. While Esau's birth stopped the gossipers from spreading rumors about Nadine's so-called disease, the rumor mill quickly cranked up again and generated a new one.

"Some of the talking heads spread untruths about many things. One was about the children allegedly not having enough food to eat. I don't believe in getting caught up in other people's business, but I felt compelled to intervene in this because I knew for a fact that Nadine's children were well fed and healthy. Whereby some people might have T-bone steaks for dinner, her children might have hamburger steak. While others might have center cut pork chops, they would simply have assorted pork chops. One day there were three additional unexpected children at Nadine's house ready for supper. Without her mumbling a word I saw her add a can of red beans, ketchup, and a little more water to stretch the spaghetti sauce she had prepared. She did not receive one complaint about it from the children. Everybody ate all that they wanted. They just dove in, smacked their lips, and enjoyed the food. I take a little something over there once a week to give Nadine a little break. Sometimes it's no more than baking a sheet pan of tea cakes for the children to eat for an afternoon snack as she prepares their dinner.

"The children look nice and neat when they go to school and to church. They don't worry about wearing new clothes because once clothes are washed, they all look the same, new or not. I am thankful for children being allowed to wear blue jeans to school because when the schools integrated, you could not tell the rich children from the poor ones. Most of the student body wore jeans to school, and her children do too. Nadine's children are doing well and I just love them all.

"I'm happy because I go out there at least once a week and I have witnessed for myself their excellent care. I'm not telling you about something that I've heard. I'm telling you, as a bona fide eyewitness, about what I know. We all need to be careful about who we listen to and who we follow. If you follow someone to a swamp and get suckered in, there too you will dwell. Haters love to create and cause problems. It seems like some people lie awake at night making up excuses as to why certain things in their lives are not the way they think they should be; therefore, they decide who they want to blame, then invite the usual group and throw a pity party. Year after year the same old lies are hashed over and over again by the same old crew, who think that their disdain for someone is not recognizable; they must be very naïve or simpletons. They are as transparent as a windowpane or a piece of clear plastic wrap. Being deceitful and deviant does not wear well on one's face. Thank God for the gift of discernment. By now, you would think that these untruths would had stopped. But oh no, whenever certain people gather, you can be assured that their favorite subjects, true or not, will reactivate and not skip a beat.

"Haters and liars can be vicious and unproductive people who need to stop throwing stones and then hiding their hands. Stones can ricochet and inflict harm on those who throw them and on others. Some haters have marched in place for years, not gaining any traction or ground, simply growing old, weary, and often waddling in their own self-imposed pity. Brakes need to be applied to this unfounded madness and they need to stop breaking the commandment of 'Thou shall not bear false witness against your neighbor.' One day, a lady told a female member of a gossiping clique that it was by the grace of God that no one had yet slapped her face all the way to the back of her head for causing so much dissension with her mouth, and if she wasn't careful, she might talk herself all the way into Hell. Wouldn't it be horrible to miss out on the glory of the Lord because of a balmy tongue? I love a quote of Dr. Martin Luther King Jr., which says 'I have decided to stick with love. Hate is too great a burden to bear.'"

When we drove up to Ms. Nadine's house, we saw the children playing dodgeball in the front yard. Ms. Nadine heard our car and came out to greet us. The children came over to the car to help bring in the items Granny had brought for them. The children were very friendly. As soon as they smelled the batch of sugar cookies, they knew that they were in for a treat. The children were full of questions for me. They first asked if I was the grandson from Philadelphia or one of the grandchildren from Ghana. I told them my name and that I live in Philadelphia. Next, they asked about the snow and if I liked playing in it. They rarely saw snow and were fascinated by it. I told them I loved to play in snow all day when I was younger, but now I mostly like having snowball fights with my friends. Then, they asked if I knew how to make snow-cream. They shared a time a couple of years ago that it snowed in their area and how much fun they had making snow-cream by using evaporated milk, sugar, lemon or vanilla flavor, and, of course, the snow. They also asked about the Liberty Bell, Ben Franklin's old post office, and Independence Hall. I told them I visited each of these places while on field trips with my school.

Nadine's children were excited about starting to get things ready for church this coming Sunday. We quickly learned that Rev. Joyner called Ms. Nadine and told her that Mr. Gerald would pick them up on the church bus at 8:30 a.m. for Sunday school and would bring them back home after the church service. The children loved to go to church and looked forward to Mr. Gerald giving each of them a piece of bubble gum when they returned home. His departing words to them would always be "Be good and I will see you bright and early next Sunday morning." Ms. Nadine was a terrific planner and she taught her children to be likewise. Some of the older girls had polished the shoes of the younger children and placed them on one side of the porch to dry in preparation for Sunday morning. Everywhere you looked, everybody was busy like little ants—busy making a contribution, no matter how large or how small, it was for the benefit of them all. It was a sight to behold, to see everything seemingly move along like clockwork.

The children asked if I would play a game of dodgeball with them. As soon as I said yes, I was immediately recruited by the girls' team in an effort to equalize the teams. The boys were up first and they proved to be very agile. Every time one of them would get out, they felt the sting and yelled out "Oh, Raspberry!" which they were substituting for a four-letter word. Two of Ms. Nadine's older boys wanted me to throw their football to check out my strength and, after attempting to catch it several times, they started calling me "Iron Man Dan" because of the force they felt when they attempted to catch the ball.

I had fun visiting Ms. Nadine and her family and wished I could have stayed longer but we were on a mission and it was about time to go. The children invited me to attend Vacation Bible School with them the week after next and hoped that I could come. I told them if I was still visiting during that time, I would be sure to see them there. Granny and I said our goodbyes and headed back to the car.

On our ride to our third visit, Granny said, "The only concern I have about Nadine and her children is that when she grows old and weary and in need of care, will they take care of her like she took care of them, showering her with tons of love? Or will she be passed around from house to house like an inconvenient chore that no one wants? I've always heard the saying that one mother can take care of eight children but eight children can't seem to take care of one mother. Jesus left a perfect example pertaining to the care of his mother as he was about to be crucified on a cross at Mount Calvary. He knew that he would not be around to take care of his mother, Mary, so before he gave up his spirit, he made sure that someone would be there for her. He asked John, one of his disciples, to take care of her, and John accepted the responsibility for her care."

CHAPTER NINE

ALFORD COVINGTON

Our next and final stop on our way to the revival was at a house that is situated directly between Beauty Grove Baptist Church and a club called the Dew Drop Inn Club. This is the home of Alford Covington, a professed nonbeliever. Granny described him as a tall, handsome, and wayward man. On our ride to his house, Granny told me that Covington did not care about what others thought of him; he just wanted to have a good time. She said often you could hear him singing, "Come on, baby, let the good times roll." He was somewhat of a narcissist and did as he pleased. He loved the women, and the women loved him. If anyone talked to him about God, they would have to get ready for a blistering cussing out, even using the Lord's name in vain. He would curse anyone up one side and down the other. I think he could outcuss a seasoned cussing sailor.

Granny said, "Covington was such a tyrant in his home until everyone walked around like they were stepping on eggshells. Many years ago, after the passing of Mrs. Covington, his bloody raw behavior escalated and he became unbearable. He showed a different face to different people; however, he was at his worst when he walked through the front door of his house. Covington showed no interest in his children, their education, or anything else they did. He refused to attend any activity they participated in at school or at church. He never attended a parent/teacher conference in his life and made it known loud and clear that he never intended too. He was well known as a person you didn't want to tangle with. When you found yourself unexpectedly in his presence, it was best for you to stand at attention, salute, and be on your merry way."

Enough Is Enough

"Your dad and Covington's oldest son were friends," said Granny. "We all called him Junior. He is such a nice fellow and you would not believe the environment he had to experience as a child. Junior and his siblings turned out well despite what they had to endure as children. Covington would constantly embarrass his children in front of their friends by severely demeaning them. He was considered to be a down-to-the-bone mean man with devilish ways. He would throw pots, pans, plates, and anything else he could get his hands on when he got upset or when he just felt like being destructive and contrary. After which, he would order his children to pick them up and wash them. Sometimes he would do this action repeatedly for hours, or until he fell asleep. One day he threw a pot, full of piping hot grits, across the kitchen, just missing his oldest son's head. It angered his son and he lifted his hands up towards his father, only to be restrained by his siblings like the archangel Michael did in the Bible. He was what some would call a humdinger, a beast of a man beyond being wicked. It was during this time that the children decided to leave their father's house to escape his physical and emotional tyrant ways. They banded together and agreed that they'd had enough of his abuse and refused to continue to be victims. They committed to supporting each other, saying, 'One for all and all for one with the blessings of our Lord and Savior Jesus Christ, forever.' This was what their late mother would often say to promote unity and strength among her children. She also would say that sometimes you have to do what you have to do. They realized that it wouldn't be easy, but they were ready and able to do their part. Their mother had been gone for a while, but the lessons she taught them about the Lord and about his goodness continued to remain with them. When the Covington siblings wanted to feel closer to their mother, they would often open her personal Bible, read her favorite passage, the 23rd Psalm, and look at the dried pink carnation flowers they had placed in it as a reminder of her unwavering love. They knew they had to step it up and step out on faith and that God would provide all of their needs."

"Granny," I said, "sometimes we don't know how good we got it until we hear someone else's story. I'm sorry they had to go through that and leave their home in order to survive."

Granny continued. "One day, not long after the children left home, Covington was sitting on his front porch and saw that his dog, Bullet, had gotten off his chain and was hastily leaving the yard. He called for him to come back and yelled, 'Come here, Bullet, come here, boy.' Bullet stopped, looked at Covington, growled, released a couple of barks, then turned his head and trotted off in the opposite direction heading straight towards the woods. The louder Covington called for him to come back, the faster Bullet ran. Bullet, too, had had enough and ran away from his oppressor. He was out of there and never to be seen again."

I said, "Wow, Granny, wow! Even the dog knew something wasn't right. I have a friend back home named Marquise who had a similar problem. Social services worked with his entire family to help resolve the situation he had been experiencing at home. He told me that the social worker assigned to his case said that the last thing social services wanted to do was break up a family unit and that they work towards finding solutions to their problems, whenever possible. He's a nice dude and a good friend. Marquise is frequently bullied at school because of things he doesn't have.

"Granny, I know my parents probably told you about the fight I had at school this past school year. Well, I was aware of Marquise's home situation and I saw how some students picked on him just for the fun of it. On the day I got in that fight, I saw one of them bullying him again and I asked him to give Marquise a break and to just leave him alone. The bully said, 'You little freshman turd, I've got something for you too.' That's when someone shoved that bully into me and he started punching me really hard. I've always been taught not to fight, but never have I been told not to defend myself. The next thing I knew, Coach Blocker, the football coach, was pulling that big bully up off the floor and taking us to the assistant principal's office to be suspended. I wish I'd handled the situation better that day. I could've asked an adult to get involved, like a school counselor, Coach Blocker, or another respected and caring adult."

"You're right," responded Granny, "sometimes we have to reach out for help."

Granny continued to talk and I listened. "One Saturday morning, a small group of people knocked on Covington's front door distributing religious literature," said Granny. "When he learned what they were doing, he became unbelievably angry and ordered them off his property. He indignantly stated that he bought the land and did not want them to set one foot on his dirt. He sent out the promise that if they came again, he was going to call the law and have them all arrested for trespassing. The evangelists with the religious literature showed self-control and began to leave his property; however, a young boy in the group, about the age of seven or eight, stopped and said, 'Pardon me, sir, God made this dirt, He made all of it. Look, read! This paper tells us that God made everything.' He paused and said, 'Where is the dirt you made, sir?' Covington became speechless and went in his house and slammed the door. The group walked away with great pride, smiling ear to ear, emphasizing the saying about "from the mouths of babes," in Matthew 21:16."

Time for Reckoning

Granny explained that as Covington got older, the crowd he partied with year after year got younger. He was much older than most of them and became known to them as "Pops."

"This is when his house became the party house," said Granny. "So many drunkards would meet up there to do whatever they wanted to do. Even tractor trailer drivers parked their rigs at his house, some with license plates from as far away as Arizona. The Covington house, which was once known, back in the day, as a nice family home, became a house of ill repute and a nuisance to the community. This spot was so popular that it caused the clubs and lounges around the area to lose money. Some of the owners almost went out of business. The people who used to hang out at the Dew Drop Inn Club started telling others about the 'good times house' and invited them to patronize what had now become known as The Covington House. When husbands could not find their wives and wives could not find their husbands, that was the first place they would go looking for their spouses. Even teens would frequent there, then leaving intoxicated or high on drugs, unable to make it home on their own. Parents were often seen pulling their children out of this foul place as others defiantly refused to leave. It became known as a place where all of the Ten Commandments were broken at one time or another. Often the neighbors referred to it as the Buttermilk Bottom. They described it as a terrible place infested with disgusting metallic-looking green blowflies."

Granny said, "The goings-on at this sinful spot quickly turned into nightmares. Houses in the area were steadily being put up for sale; however, no one was willing to purchase them because of the location. The Covington House was too close for comfort. Things got way out of hand. The police sent a cease and desist order, to no avail. The house was under constant surveillance and later raided. Covington was charged with multiple violations, handcuffed, and taken to the county jail. He ended up having to go to court and stand in front of a judge."

The judge read the charges brought against him, then asked, "How do you plead to these charges, Mr. Covington, guilty or not guilty?"

In a raspy voice he said, "Not guilty, Your Honor, sir."

The judge said, "Well, how do you explain all of these charges that go back for many years on your rap sheet?"

Covington responded, "It's not my fault, Your Honor; people do awful things, then put the blame on me all the time. I'm just trying to make it in this old world, the best way I can, Your Honor, sir."

The judge replied, "Who are you referring to, Mr. Covington? No one is standing here before me for a ruling except for you."

Covington stated, "I can't name them right now, Your Honor—their names escape me at this time—but there are a lot of people out to get me."

The judge said, "Well, concerning the house in question, who owns it, you or the people you say are out to get you?"

Covington replied, "I do, Your Honor. I own the house. I bought and paid for it by myself. No one ever gave me anything in my life. I've had to work hard for whatever I got. My name was nowhere to be found on my parents' will and everything of any value not listed in the will was taken by my low-down, thieving, wolf-in-sheep's-clothing brother. You know they say that there is a thief in every family, Your Honor."

The judge responded, "So, Mr. Covington, the responsibility of the house that operates 24 hours, 365 days a year, at 1948 Narrow Way Drive belongs exclusively to you?"

"Yes, sir, Your Honor," said Covington. "That's my house. I paid it off all by myself several years ago and burned the mortgage papers in my fireplace. Your Honor, I should not be here in court. I've been an upstanding citizen in this community for many years. I'm a good guy. A few of my friends come by to check up on me from time to time. They might get a little loud, but they don't mean any harm, sir. I don't bother nobody, just ask anybody," said Covington.

"Mr. Covington," said the judge, "the court tried to work with you, and gave you many opportunities to avoid charges pertaining to the happenings at your residence by sending you warnings and that cease and desist order. I have been notified that the order was properly served and nothing was changed. It has been reported and verified that many of your neighbors are intimidated to even walk past your house in fear of what might come flying out your door, including but not limited to vulgar-laced profanity, people fighting with knives, crowbars, and at times, the presence of handguns. Also, they are fearful of being hit by a variety of household items and other unknown objects. So, Mr. Covington, is there anything you wish to say on your behalf to the court before I rule on your case?"

He responded, "Yes, sir, Your Honor."

The judge replied, "What do you have to say?"

"Your Honor," said Covington, "I throw myself on the mercy of the court. Please, sir, I beg you to have mercy on me. I'm a veteran, served my country well, and I was honorably discharged. I'm an old man with many infirmities and there are times I can hardly put one foot in front of the other without stumbling and falling down. What is a fellow in my physical condition to do? I beg you to please have mercy on me, sir, and spare me from going to prison."

The judge paused for a while and said, "Mr. Covington, you never know who is watching or keeping tabs on you. Often, it is those you least suspect. With all of the heinous reports I have received and thoroughly reviewed pertaining to your obnoxious ways and the nasty corrupt behavior of your patrons, I have no doubt that you are guilty as charged. You asked for mercy from the court, Mr. Covington?"

Covington replied, "Yes, sir, Your Honor, I beg you to please have mercy on me."

The judge continued, "The only mercy I have is for your neighbors for having to tolerate you and your kind for such a long time. I can hardly believe, after all that you've been found guilty of, you stand here and have the audacity to ask for mercy. Mr. Covington, unfortunately for you, your mercy has an expiration date as of today. It's time for a new chapter in your life, that's why I'm sentencing you according to the new guidelines pertaining to habitual offenders."

The judge summoned two court bailiffs to take Covington out of the courtroom and ordered him to be transported to the State Pen for no less than two years and for no more than five years. The judge said, "What is this world coming to?" He shook his head, wiped away a tear, then said, "It's been a long time coming, Mr.

Covington, and I wish you well." He signed the order, then banged his gavel on the large shiny mahogany desk as he vacated the bench and went to his chambers.

Granny commented that not a single person from Covington's family or the community had shown up in support of him. He was escorted out of the courtroom wearing a bright orange baggy jumpsuit, flip-flops, and white socks. His head was bowed with his hands and legs shackled with chains like a wild animal unfit to be around civilized people. He was surrounded in his own world of narcissism with his three best pronoun friends: Me, Myself, and I. He thought it was all about him and that's precisely why he ended up in the State Penitentiary. He had the mindset that rules were not made for him, but for everybody else. He did what he wanted to do, when he wanted to do it, without any consideration for anyone else. He just didn't care about anybody or anything.

I said, "Granny, I wonder what caused him to treat everybody so mean?"

She answered, "I do not know and I often wonder if he even knows why himself. Over the years, some people are angry with each other and when somebody asks them what they are angry about, they can't seem to recall."

I said, "He must have felt lonely standing there all by himself. I've always been told that it's good to have friends and that doesn't necessarily mean you have to have a lot of them. My parents say that all you really need are a few good friends."

CHAPTER TEN

YOU REAP WHAT YOU SOW

Granny said that after Covington's conviction, it was time for him to be placed in a highly secured prison van. In front of the van were two state trooper cars and there were also two of them behind it. They had a convoy with flashing blue lights warning others to keep their distance. All of the troopers were heavily armed and wearing bulletproof vests. Their mission was to keep the prisoners from escaping and to escort the van to its destination. Covington thought this was a bit too much for somebody like him. "Why all the pomp and circumstance?" The van door was opened for him to get in and there sat two men. One of them looked to be in his early twenties while the other appeared to be in his late thirties or early forties. Covington learned by having a brief conversation with a bailiff that one was convicted of murder and the other was convicted of robbery, kidnapping, and murder.

In an authoritative voice, Covington said to one of the bailiffs, "I think you put me in the wrong van, man.

I'm not like them; you need to check your papers to see if you made a mistake."

The bailiff took a long, hard, thorough look at the orders, and said to him firmly, "No, sir," and then he laughed. "No mistakes were made, you are exactly where you belong, according to the order signed by the Honorable Judge A.L. Covington Jr." Covington was shocked to hear who had signed the order and asked the bailiff to repeat the judge's name. He obliged and repeated it. It was Covington's now-grown son. Junior had been out of his life for so long that he didn't even recognize him.

Hearing the conversation, one of the prisoners injected himself into it by saying, "Oh, I see that ol' hanging judge got you too. Who does he think he is, sitting up there in his long black robe, looking down on us like he's so high and mighty, passing judgment on us? He's no good for his people, putting us in prison for such a long time. He went off to college and got a little education and now he thinks he's better than us. In my book, he's just an educated fool. He must have never had it hard, like me. I had to fight for everything I ever got in life, even for a crust of stale bread. You can look at him and tell he's always lived a life of privilege, born to parents who not only put a pure silver spoon in his mouth, but he probably also had a pure silver fork and a pure silver knife. If I ever get out of prison, I've got something to settle with him. I'm going to hunt him down like a vicious, two-headed, venomous cottonmouth snake."

One of the guards said to the complaining prisoner, "That's enough. He's just doing his job. I sat in during your trial and it's not his fault that you started killing neighborhood pets when you were a child and never felt any remorse for your actions. Any person in his right mind could have told you, even back then, that this kind of behavior was a loud cry for a big intervention in your life. Unfortunately, you did not get the help you needed and your sick behavior escalated into taking the life of a human being. When you get to the state penitentiary, it's like you are on a big taxpayer scholarship. You get free housing, utilities, food, clothing, medical, dental, and psychological services. Everything is free, except for one super important thing—your freedom."

"At the penitentiary," Granny stated, "the months slowly passed and turned into even slower years. This is when Covington was forced to face the reality that even his so-called friends, people he thought he could depend upon to visit occasionally, turned their backs on him. Two times a year, however, during the Christmas and Easter seasons, he noticed the pattern of local church groups visiting and bearing gifts, then returning to an out-of-sight, out-of-mind self-imposed exile until the seasons rolled around again. He described them as being limited, seasonal, part-time Christians, bringing forth a pair of socks for Christmas and, during the Easter season, a second pair to make themselves feel good. Some of the church groups would invite reporters from a variety of television stations to record and show on the airwaves what they were doing for the less fortunate.

Covington did his time and was released. There, waiting at the gate of the state prison, was one of his old drinking buddies who had purchased Covington's favorite whisky, Crown Royal. He immediately told him to take a swig for old time's sake and to let the good times roll; without hesitation, he did. As a matter of fact, the driver and Covington were both inebriated by the time they got home. The old routine continued like a revolving door; it didn't skip a beat. Prison had not rehabilitated him. However, during the time he was away, the community experienced solace and had a chance to breathe peacefully."

Fair-Weather Friends

Granny said, "Covington would get his pension check and he and his friends would drink alcohol until the money was gone. Even young women would go to him, smile, flirt, and borrow money, which they never intended to repay. Like a blockhead, he fell for it every time, swallowing the bait, hook, line, and sinker. He was an easy target and everyone knew it. At one point, he was surviving on food such as sardines, potted meat, and saltine crackers for breakfast, lunch, and dinner. During this time, he was suspected of going into a neighbor's house, and taking two small field rabbits, who were adopted as pets, and some rice. The neighbor returned home only to find that the rabbits were missing and some of the rice from the kitchen cabinet had spilled on the floor. He did not confront Covington, for he knew what he would be up against, and believed some things were best left alone. There are times in life when you have to choose your battles. You can't fight about everything and he was not interested in turning a molehill into a mountain.

"When Covington's money ran out, so did his fair-weather friends and he would not see them again until it was time for him to get his next check.

"One time, Covington's money was getting low so he went deep into the woods to a moonshiner and brought some corn liquor. He was sold a quart and it made him violently ill; he was hospitalized for five days. The doctor said that he must have gotten hold of an extremely toxic jar of liquor known as rotgut. He also said that people don't seem to get the fact that the word 'intoxication' contains the word 'toxic,' which means poison. When people consume liquor, they are actually putting poison into their own bodies.

"Covington was released from the hospital and was in dire need of home care," said Granny. "He had alienated so many people until no one was willing to help him." Granny also shared her apprehension about helping him too. So she prayed about the situation and developed a plan of action. She informed him that she would help him on the condition that he would not curse around her and that she would talk about her God whenever she wanted to, with or without his permission. She informed him that the first time their verbal agreement is broken, she would be withdrawing her services. He agreed to the conditions and, with that, she added him to her sick and shut-in list.

"Danny," Granny said, "sometimes we can observe someone's life experience and know that it is not the life we want for ourselves. We can learn from the experience of others."

When we arrived at Mr. Covington's house to drop off his meal, I felt as if I already knew him. He was sitting outside on his porch, dressed as if he was getting ready to go somewhere. He said, "Hey, Sister Bretta Jones, I'm glad you came a little earlier today. I've been looking forward all day to eating your chicken, vegetable, and wide noodle soup. I can hardly wait to eat it. It's always delicious and it helps me to feel revitalized." He sat down, ate most of the soup, and left some of the broth in the bottom of the bowl. I thought he was going to drink it. Instead, he broke off a piece of the Ezekiel bread, and sopped up the remaining broth in the bowl, making it bone dry. Feeling full and content, Covington asked for a ride to the church so he could hear "those boys down there play that music." Granny was receptive and responded, "Certainly. Come on and let's go."

CHAPTER ELEVEN

COVINGTON OFF TO REVIVAL

We got in the car, then off to Beauty Grove Baptist Church we went. I relinquished the front passenger seat to Mr. Covington and sat directly behind him. I wanted to monitor his behavior. He had his hair combed and slicked back. A thin narrow mustache adorned his upper lip. His suit was wrinkled and obviously too large, but he didn't seem to care. He also had on an excessive amount of a supersweet cologne. A lot of the smell left the car when the windows were rolled down. I wondered to myself, as he engaged in conversation with Granny, just who was he trying to impress. I thought, *surely not my Granny. She is definitely off-limits.* I wanted him to behave himself because I didn't want to have to take matters into my own hands. When it comes to my Granny, I would not hesitate to protect her and say to him that he needs to slow his roll, stay in his lane, and to leave my Granny alone!

We drove up to the church. Cars were parked everywhere. The service was just starting when we entered. Mr. Covington came in last and sat in the very last row, as if not wanting to draw any attention to himself. That did not last very long. People began to whisper and point in his direction. They had a hard time believing that this ornery old man who had such an extreme disdain for the Lord was sitting up in the church. It was packed and you had to look for a seat.

One of Granny's friends said, "Come on over here, Bretta. You sit with us and over there is a seat for your grandson." I was happy with my seat assignment. I got to sit next to Phoebe Joyner, the pastor's cute daughter. Just about everybody was standing up, singing, clapping, their hands, or stomping their feet on the wooden plank floor. I saw that people worshipped in different ways. It was a lot different from my church back home. One person began to run around in circles inside the church. Another one fainted and the ladies of the church gathered around and began to fan her. Some of them wept openly, while others spoke in unknown tongues (1 Corinthians 14:2-19). Some repeatedly called on the name of Jesus. There were people who shouted as well as those who sat still. Personal testimonies came from parted lips as some sat quietly and meditated. They had it going on up in there. It was rocking. I loved the music, but I just sat there trying to look cool and unimpressed. I surprised myself, however, when I noticed that I was tapping my foot to the rhythm of the music and did not miss a single beat, so I stopped.

The news of the revival traveled fast and people came out to be a part of it. I just looked at them, determined not to be like them. No way, nothing was going to make me lose control and act like them; oh no, not me. The praise portion of the service was over and now the pastor was about to preach the Word. He began the sermon by saying that we all are sinners who need to repent if we want to go to Heaven to see our Savior's face. He preached about the many benefits of being born again. Then I thought, "Here we go again, talking about that born again stuff." He preached and preached about the benefits of being saved and becoming a child of God until he almost lost his voice. Sweat began to drip from his face. He didn't seem to mind; he came prepared to take care of each and every drop. It didn't bother him at all; he just wiped it off with a long white towel that was slung across his shoulder and continued to preach. He preached himself happy and cut a step or two. As he preached, the musicians were with him all the way, playing certain notes to emphasize the spoken Word. You could tell that some of them also felt the Spirit stirring up in their souls. The sounds they made with their instruments had to be a gift from God.

That old worn church was rocking and reeling with the presence of the Lord. Suddenly, I found myself listening to the sermon and began to realize that this born again stuff was real. Then I started telling myself excuses as to why I was not ready to dedicate my life to God, when a feeling came upon me and took over. All I could think about was what is this thing upon me? By this time, the pastor was calling for the unsaved to come to the mourner's bench to accept Jesus into our lives. He asked God to look beyond our faults and to see our needs. All I could think about was how can I get out of this place?

My need at that moment was to find a way to escape Beauty Grove Baptist Church. People were heading to the mourner's bench in droves and I was going in the opposite direction to the side door. I didn't want any part of that Holy Ghost thing; it wasn't for me and I could get saved when I got a little older. All I wanted to do was make a quick exit out of there.

I glanced over toward the last row of the church. There, I surprisingly saw Mr. Covington rise up from his seat and start walking down the red-carpeted center aisle speaking in a raspy, but booming voice, saying, "Lord, I am a sinner in need of your mercy. Thank you for looking beyond my faults and seeing my needs. Help me to be saved. Please, Father, forgive me of my many trespasses. I need you in my life, dear Father, and I yield, I yield, I yield totally to you." He hobbled on down to the mourner's bench, continuing to pray and calling on the name of Jesus. It was stunning seeing him do that and he sounded sincere. His earlier goal of going to revival to hear the music had now been transformed to a different mission. He was going to the mourner's bench in an attempt to hit a home run for his salvation. He appeared to be very familiar with the process.

Instantly, I realized that the spirit of God was upon me. I unexpectedly found myself headed to the mourner's bench. Next, I found myself down there too on my knees, with Covington at my left and Pinky on my right. The pastor's wife knelt beside me and said, "Call on the name of Jesus;" I called on His name. She told me to call Him a little harder; I called His name harder. Then she said, "Call on Him like you mean it and ask Him to forgive you of your sins" and I did. When

I accepted the Holy Spirit into my life, Granny, with her arthritic knees, began to step high in her high-heel shoes, with her shoulders reared back and her head held high. Everybody was saying that my Granny looked like a proud drum major for Jesus Christ. Church service was now over for Thursday night.

Many people stayed afterwards and talked. The pastor said that God was pleased and smiling down on us and that we received the ultimate gift: eternal life.

Oh, how awesome and exhilarating it is to be called a child of God. This group consisted of the old as well as the young, tall and short, stout and slim, loud mourners as well those whose voices you could barely hear and everything else in between. It was said that we looked like a freshly planted flower garden with the likes of Covington, Pinky, others, and me.

Mr. Covington briefly walked away and someone asked the pastor, "How can a cantankerous, scornful, mean old man like Alford Covington be saved with all of his wrongdoings?"

Rev. Joyner responded, "God is a good God who accepts us just as we are. He does not discriminate."

I entered into the church that evening like a regular person, as if I was on a common rowboat, but after accepting God as my personal Savior, I felt elevated and sailed out of there like I was on my Heavenly Father's great yacht. My life had been lifted to a higher plane. My biggest concern now was, when I got back home, would my friends, especially the girls, accept me as I am?

It was time to go back to Granny's house, but first we had to take Mr. Covington home. Pinky passed us on the highway as if she were in a big hurry. She drove beyond the bright red flashing light emanating from the Dew Drop Inn Club sign. Granny, Mr. Covington, and I had been holding our breath, but could now exhale. But then Pinky's car made a U-turn in the middle of the road and the right-hand blinker came on, signaling that the Dew Drop Inn Club was on her radar. No one said a word. It's amazing how loud silence can sound.

We continued on to our destination. No lights had been left on at his house, not even the porch light. Covington started talking about regrets in his life, especially the ones about his children and how his ungodly ways caused him to be a King of Sin. He spoke of how his life was surrounded by darkness, just like that dark house he was about to enter, and how it was nobody's fault but his own. He said light is so important in the life of a Christian, but that sinners are in love with the cloak of darkness. That's when many of them love to sin, thinking that no one will know about it but them. He said that he knew because he had been a big-time sinner. He took full responsibility and made no excuses.

Mr. Covington said, "Bretta, it's so nice that your grandson is spending some time with you. I'm a grandfather many times over and I have never laid eyes on any of my grandchildren. I've only seen pictures of them." Granny told him that tonight was a new beginning and that he could make a difference in being accepted by his children and grandchildren.

Mr. Covington said that he'd gone to church, sat in the last pew to hear the young people play their music, and that they had not disappointed him. He continued, "They played really well, but the sweetest sounds I heard were the words of God. I know that one day if I want to see my Lord and Savior's face, then according to John 3:6 and 7, I must be born again." He got out of the car, did a quick shout, and gave a hallelujah praise, stating, "I once was lost, but now I'm found, was blind but now I see." He thanked God for all of his goodness and mercies and for breaking his bondage. He said good night and headed towards the front door of his house. Granny aimed the high beam car lights towards his front door so he could easily see to unlock it. His parting words were that he'd had a great time at the revival service and asked if she could please pick him up the same time tomorrow. He said, "Sister Bretta, I'm still in the middle of tempta-tion. When I come out my front door, I have a decision to make every day. If I go to the left, I'll end up at the Dew Drop Inn Club, or if I go to the right, I'll go in the direction of Beauty Grove Baptist Church. I need and welcome your help, my dear sister."

She said, "Gladly. We'll see you tomorrow at the same time, my dear brother."

We drove off and I began to quiz Granny about Mr. Covington's prayer and his understanding of the Bible. After the service, people had been asking him biblical questions left and right. They asked him questions about things that never crossed my mind. He answered all of them in an authoritative way. I asked her how he could know so much about the Bible already when he was just at the mourner's bench next to me. She paused and said that it was her understanding that the Gospel was not new to him and that, many years ago, he was a well-known child preacher and had somehow lost his way. People used to call him a prodigy. When he was a younger man, he was in high demand, preaching up and down the East Coast. He even accepted invitations to deliver sermons at packed arenas overseas. She said, "That raspy sound in his voice is probably the result of him powerfully preaching the Word of God for many years. I don't know what happened in his life to cause him to fall out of favor with God, but I am thankful he's back. God has recovered one of his lost sheep."

CHAPTER TWELVE

HARRIET'S BIG SURPRISE

Friday

This morning when my friend "Redcap" crowed, I jumped up out of bed. I got up early so I could do something special for Granny. I had it all planned out, but first, I took my shower and then hurried into the kitchen. I'd been watching her cook, and had learned my way around her kitchen. Hopefully, I'd picked up some of her extraordinary culinary skills. I fried some applewood smoked bacon, scrambled some eggs with cheese, and heated the maple syrup in the microwave oven while I put the French toast on the griddle. They were topped with her favorite fruit: huckleberries and sliced bananas. I poured her a tall glass of cold sweet milk and topped off the breakfast with a cup of hot tea sweetened with local honey. Also on the tray, I put a warm damp facecloth so that she could wash her face and hands, along with a small paper cup filled with half water and half mouthwash if she cared to refresh her mouth.

Everything turned out great and I served her breakfast in bed. Granny was elated and shed a few tears of joy, wiped her eyes, and ate every bit of her food. If someone saw Granny's plate at the end of breakfast, it would be hard to guess what was on the menu. Nothing was left on the plate that could be contributed to the slop bucket for the big sow Granny named Harriet. Granny said to be especially kind to Harriet and to add some extra food from the feed sack, stored in the barn, to the slop. She also instructed me to be sure to give her five ears of dried corn on the cob. I thought to myself, *why is Granny having Harriet fed so much food?* If anything, I thought, she might need to cut back a bit. I got everything together as I was instructed. Since I started spending time on the small farm, I'd learned the importance of following directions. I told Granny not to worry and that she was queen for the day and to rest. I am a quick learner and I knew exactly what I needed to do.

Granny was an excellent teacher. She was kind, firm but fair. I cleaned the kitchen, then went out back to take care of the animals. At the door, waiting, was my friend "Redcap." He shadowed me as I performed my chores. The chickens had already been fed, but "Redcap" stayed close to me, still wanting for something else. I reached in my pocket and there it was—some cracked corn for once my foe, but now my friend, "Redcap."

We didn't have much to do today and I looked forward to doing the chores I once complained about when I first stepped foot on that soil. Work gave me a sense of self-worth and I liked feeling that way. I was delighted to feed and give the animals all that they needed.

The hog pen was the last feeding stop on my list. I looked in the pen, gearing up to feed Harriet, but she was not in her usual spot. I turned and looked under the shade tree and that is where I saw her and witnessed the miracle of birth. She was in the process of becoming the mother of ten little piglets and, as they arrived, they nestled closely to their mother. Granny hit the nail on the head again. She knew of Harriet's condition and how she needed extra feed so she could be healthy and able to take care of her newly acquired responsibility. I saw God's Word being actualized as it is laid out in Genesis about being fruitful and multiplying. First it was just Harriet; now it was Harriet plus ten more. That was an epic increase. It appeared that there would not be a shortage of swine in this world and that was part of God's plan, for all life forms on this Earth.

I choked up a bit when I realized the importance of my dad's job, working long hours as a research zoologist, taking care of God's creations, as He commanded. Trying to stop them from becoming extinct could be a difficult job, for God was depending on man to be the caretakers of the Earth and all of its inhabitants. My dad often says it's somewhat like they say about putting the fox in charge of the henhouse, for man had precipitated a lot of the problems, which had caused certain animals and certain plants to become extinct from the face of this Earth.

The cantaloupe seeds Granny told me to plant when I first arrived were beginning to sprout in the container that was watered. There was no sign of life in the pot not watered. Life would not exist without God supplying us with water. It doesn't just show up from a faucet in the kitchen, the bathroom, or from an outside spigot or pump. God supplies water for the entire world. Man cannot do that and he never will. No living thing can survive without water, not even an enormous elephant or a single blade of grass. All living things need water to survive.

This was a slow, calming day, except for Harriet's big surprise. Granny and I had an enjoyable time as we looked at old photos of the family and some people of the community. There were pictures of my dad and Aunt Claire when they were children. My Grandpa Thaddeus, who passed away when I was ten, and Dad looked very similar in many of the pictures. Granny had to look at some of them for a while before knowing who was who in the photos. In one worn photo was a lady with long, silky, dark hair and high cheekbones. Her name was not readily known, but they took pride in calling her one of their relatives. Snapshot pictures were taken during Christmas, Easter, and May Day activities. Granny loved a particular picture of my dad and Aunt Claire with Professor Taylor standing between them in front of the now old abandoned school. She talked joyfully about the good ol' days when the school and the church were used for many community activities. She gave high marks to the Professor and Mrs. Taylor, who cared about all of the children at Spring Hope Elementary School and were very instrumental in helping them to become their very best. The Taylors, along with the other dedicated faculty members, were top-notch educators and well respected. They believed in the total child, therefore, causing the children to believe in themselves.

I loved it when Granny told stories about how things used to be in the old days. Many of them were mind-blowing and thought-provoking. We stayed on the front porch a long time that day. I was on the swing and she was sitting in a rocking chair keeping a steady beat. It began to get really hot. The meteorologist had forecasted that the temperature would be in the mid-90s. We continued to sit there rocking, swinging, and eating frozen slices of yummy peaches she had taken out of her deep freezer. She loved to talk about her school days. She said that when she went to school, they started out with a devotion and usually sang the hymn "Without Him I Could Do Nothing," followed by reciting the Pledge of Allegiance and The Lord's Prayer. Granny said when they said the word "Amen," school was officially in session and ready for business.

Their schoolhouse, as it was called back in the day, didn't have a cafeteria. They took their lunch to school or didn't eat until they returned home that afternoon. One of the teachers observed that a lot of the children were not eating lunch and came up with the idea of each child bringing in a cup of some type of beans, peas, carrots, tomatoes, rice, or anything else they could contribute to make a large pot of soup. Seasonings such as ham bones, ham hocks, or even a piece of fatback were always welcomed. Whatever the children brought to school went into the pot. One day a student brought in a cup of diced sweet potatoes, and another one brought in a cup of raw chicken fat. Those items also went into the pot. Everything was worthy and accepted. The pot was placed on the potbelly stove, which was also used to heat the classroom. A large amount of water, enough to cover the ingredients plus a little extra, was added to ensure that everyone could be served. They never knew exactly what to call it, because it all depended on what the families could spare that day. So they started to call it "mystery soup." All morning long, as they did their classwork, they looked forward to smelling the appetizing aroma of the soup, especially when the smell signaled that the soup was ready. When it was time to eat, they would line up, holding the cups that once contained the ingredients that were now in the big soup pot. On the day that the little boy contributed the diced sweet potatoes, the children got all excited about wanting to get a piece of it in their cup. Granny said her teacher, Miss Smith, also had a piece of it in her cup. She made sure that her students were full, had an active recess, then worked them hard to bring out their best.

CHAPTER THIRTEEN

FREE WITH NO PLACE TO GO

Granny shared a lot of stories about our family history. If I had not sat down and engaged her in conversation, I would have missed out on an important oral history. I'm going to write it down for future generations. I am glad we had time to talk. I've been told many times that we don't learn when we are talking and we need to listen more. We were designed with two ears and one mouth; that should tell us something. I enjoyed our talks. I learned so much from her during my stay. I was surprised that Granny had such a large stockpile of knowledge stored up inside of her. She shared stories that she remembered being told when she was a child by her great-grandmother. That would be five generations back from me.

Granny said that when the slaves were freed, my great-great-great-grandma was five years old. She remembered when the Union soldiers came to the plantation in a cavalcade, on horseback. They were told that slavery was over and that they were free. They were also told to prepare a feast for a historic celebration and that they would return for them with a chariot to take them far away from the plantation. They cooked some of the miss's chickens, smoked hams, and as a special treat, they roasted several guineas. She said that a guinea hen looks similar to a chicken but they are dark-flesh birds and are native to Africa. A large pot of rice along with a variety of vegetables was part of the celebration. They knocked down the door to the storehouse, got supplies, and baked cakes and pies. They also baked their favorite, sweet potato bread, which is like a sweet potato pie without a crust. They cooked, ate, and celebrated as they waited for a chariot to come and then grew worried as darkness began to arrive with no chariot or Union soldiers in sight. They were finally free, but with no place to go. Can you imagine the terror they must have felt? That was when reality set in that the landowners and the newly freed slaves needed each other in order to survive and that they had to work together. That was the beginning of sharecropping, which was one step up from slavery.

My Grandpa Thaddeus's father was a tobacco sharecropper, which meant that he and his family lived and worked on land that belonged to someone else. They would be responsible for the plants throughout the entire process, from the seeds to the tobacco auction warehouse. The money would be shared between the landowner and my great-grandpa. I was told about how he wanted his children to get a good education and he worked hard to buy some land to help ensure their future. Granny said that he would often recall how, one day, when he was a school-age child, he got up early and started getting ready for school, when the landowner came by their shack and told his father to keep his children home from school that day because he had some work for them to do. Frustration and disappointment ran through him. They went to the cotton field to pick what is known as scattered cotton, which were bits and pieces of cotton left on the stalks after the initial harvest, along with newly emerged cotton. He wanted to go to school and it was especially heartbreaking as he watched a school bus pick up the landowner's children from the fields he had to work. To add insult to a newly inflicted wound, the children on the bus would put down the windows and shout out insults, including calling them the "N" word.

He was already flaming hot about their mistreatment and, even though he would have had to walk three miles to school one way while the landowner's children rode a state-purchased school bus, he still had a yearning to get a good education. The two schools were in the same community, less than a mile apart. The white students rode to school on a large new bus; however, the children of color had to walk for miles to their school in all types of weather. My great-great-great-grandfather's school was built out of old wooden planks and the other school was built out of red bricks. When it rained, large pots were stationed around the classroom to catch water that dripped from the leaky roof. There was no inside plumbing, so they had to use an outhouse behind the school; of course, no outhouses were visible on the grounds of the white school. Books, maps, and other educational materials were first used by the children at the white school, then passed down to their school, often after they'd been heavily soiled and damaged. He said the only thing that helped him cope with the situation at that time was that he would often listen to his elders talk about his ancestors from his native Africa. They would tell the children about their intellect. My African ancestors were great mathematicians, scientists, and physicians, and excelled in many other areas. Not only were they very intelligent people, some of them were kings and queens of nations. The elders were great educators. They passed down pertinent information they learned about their ancestors, which was not yet taught in the history books at schools. It was a privilege for him to go to school and he challenged himself day after day to learn something new. He could often be seen concentrating on learning new spelling words or practicing his times tables as he walked the three miles back home down the dusty road leading to his shack. He was a young man preparing himself for a big mission and when the time presented itself, he wanted to be ready to accept it. He had also learned in his Sunday school class about God creating us in his own image, and that, one day with His help, he was determined to make a difference in the lives of his people.

"Danny," said Granny, "a good education is so important. Do you know it used to be against the law for our people to learn how to read? That's why, when I hear about disturbances at school and the talk about how some students put their heads down on the desk, cover up with their jackets, and go to sleep is disturbing. We had to fight hard and some people died for us to have the right to get an education." I could listen to Granny all day long, sharing stories about my ancestors. She was such an excellent storyteller. When she talked about them, I felt as if I could see them in vivid color. I've always loved her and I know she loves me unconditionally, but it's amazing when you think you know everything about someone and you really don't. It's probably due to not wanting to take the time to listen. That's what happened with me and Miss Bertha Mae Brown. She always wanted to tell me things, but I did not want to listen to her conversation. I'm glad I took time to listen to my Granny for she has shared with me an abundance of valuable information. She is very intelligent and there is more to her than meets the eye. I was way off base and way out there in left field when I underestimated the magnitude of her strength, faithfulness, and wisdom.

I had once overheard a snippet about an infamous baseball cap and asked her to share the story with me. She said that the story about the baseball cap was painful to tell. She shared that a carload of men, who didn't look like us, forced a lady's son into a car. The men rode around in the back woods and did some target shooting. One of the bullets was used to shoot a hole in the bill of her young son's baseball cap. The men ran out of bullets and went to Mullins to buy some more. They sent the boy into the store to make the purchase. The clerk behind the counter refused to sell him bullets, saying that he was underage and not allowed to purchase them. Somehow, the police became aware of the situation at hand and took the young boy to the police station to talk with him. He said, in all the years he had been in law enforcement, he had never seen anything like that and that he was keeping the baseball cap with the bullet hole in the bill in his office. Nothing was ever done to the carload of men, and for them, it was business as usual; however, the boy's mother felt that the incident was too close for comfort and sent her son to live with his father in a different state. Apparently, one of the men must have felt some remorse. During the Christmas season that year, he stopped by the mother's house and gave her a five-pound bag of oranges. Granny said that the thought of him giving that mother a small bag of oranges, with no apology, in exchange for the pure terror the young boy endured, sickened her to the core. The boy's mother accepted the oranges and put them directly in the slop bucket and fed them to the hogs.

I still had a lot of questions for her, but it was getting late and close to the time for the revival service. We had to eat supper, tidy up ourselves, and pick up Mr. Covington. The closer we got to the time for revival service, the more excited I became. I could hardly wait to join in with my church family to rejoice and praise the Lord. However, I had one other question that I knew most people had to ponder to come up with an answer, which left me feeling unsure of the correct answer. Since being on her small farm and doing the chores of feeding the chickens and collecting the eggs, I wanted to know, which came first, the chicken or the egg? Without hesitation, she instructed me to go in the house and bring out my Bible.

I did, then Granny said, "Danny, I want you to read Genesis 1:11-12 and 24-31, and there you should find your answer." I did and the answer was right there, staring me straight in my face about how God created everything, from the beginning, with its own seeds to help keep the Earth replenished. So, she asked, what's the answer to your question? I responded that I believe that the chicken was the creation and that the eggs were the seeds; therefore, the chicken came first.

CHAPTER FOURTEEN

THE SUBCONSCIOUS

It was almost time for us to leave the house. Like clockwork, I knew Granny would say to be sure to use the restroom before we left. It didn't matter where we were going, she always made the same request of me. I asked her why was it so important that I used it at home and emphasized that there was an abundance of bathrooms along the way and, if the need should arise, I could use one of them. She paused and seemed to be thinking about something deeply disturbing. She told me that when she was a child, those were exactly the words her mother would always say to her because of the lack of restroom facilities for African Americans.

Granny said, "When we left home and if we needed to relieve ourselves, many times we had to hold it until we got back home. It was not unusual to see urine running down the legs of young African American children who could not hold it any longer. Some of the men, however, would go to the side of a building or stand behind a tree to take care of this basic human need. The women had it harder for they would squat behind an open car door, using it as a shield. When you traveled on the highways in the South, restroom breaks were usually made along the side of rural roads and they would hide themselves behind bushes and trees. They had to hurry and get back in the car before another car came their way or the owner of the land spotted them on his property."

"Lord have mercy," said Granny, "it's amazing how we hold on to certain things that happened so many years ago, not realizing that it is still a part of us in our subconscious. Having two separate water fountains usually gets the most attention. However, everyone from birth to death has the same need to eat, drink, and to eliminate to maintain life. How did we get through it? It had to have been by the grace of our Lord and Savior Jesus Christ."

She then perked up and told me about a day when she was about five years old, and her mother took her to a day job she had gotten. When they arrived, her mother wanted to show her something. She opened a door and everything in that room was big and sparkling white.

"That was the first time I had ever laid eyes on an indoor bathroom," said Granny. "All I had ever known were chamber pots, which had to be emptied, basins, washtubs, and outside smelly toilets where waste eliminations piled up day after day. There was no running water. The sight of the room Mama pointed out drew me in to sit up there on that big white commode and I christened it. It was an experience I shall always remember. So, that discriminating childhood experience of not being considered worthy enough by some to use certain public facilities continues to linger deeply within me. The lady whose toilet I used was a very nice person. But during that time of my life, if she knew and had approved of it being used by a little African American child like me, she might have been callously ridiculed by her peers. Her name was Miss Ellie and as many would say, she was sweeter than a slice of pecan pie. Thus, the secret of me using her commode was buried deeply in my brain. That was between Mama and me. That's probably why over the years I have continued to say, even to my children when they were young, 'Use the bathroom before we leave the house.' Thank you, Danny, for bringing it to my attention. Well, that's enough now about me and the old days and I thank God for His love, care, and deliverance throughout the years and I'm grateful my mother did not deny me the opportunity to use it."

Granny said, "Even with certain laws, there are ways you can still be denied. For example, African American people at one time had to get their food from eating establishments through a back door or a window. One day, my cousin Myrtle and I wanted a hot dog but had to order at the window. Then time passed and the laws changed. It was then lawful for us to go inside to eat; however, sticking up from the floor in front of the counter were bolted-down metal posts minus the stool seats on top. Whites were sitting in the booths, which sent a loud and clear message of, you are legally allowed to come in, order, and pay for your food, but if you were African American there would be no place for you to sit down and eat it. We knew the booths were primarily there to accommodate the white population. Thus, we had to get our food 'to go.'"

Granny continued, "One man said that, even after the laws changed, he continued to order his food from the back window. He knew the cooks in the kitchen and they would stack his plate very high. They would pile enough food on his plate to easily feed a family of four. This man knew the value of a dollar and, by cutting certain corners, he was fortunate enough to send all of his children to college. On Saturday nights, just before it was time for the crossroad store to close, he would go there to buy all of the fish that the owner did not sell. He would get them for almost nothing. It was a win-win situation for both of them. That was good for him and good for the owner who did not reopen his store again until the following Monday morning. The savvy man and his family had fish for dinner at a very reasonable price and the store owner didn't have to clean out any smelly, decaying fish left in the bin come Monday morning. This man was often asked how he was able to do so much for his family. His answer was that he thanked God for being so good to him and his family, that he used whatever He bestowed upon them to the best of his ability. He said that he is so thankful for his brain and that he used it to help accomplish his goals. He calls it, the act of 'working his head.'"

Granny and I talked all the way to Mr. Covington's house. When we arrived, he was sitting on the edge of his front porch, waiting for us to come. The porch light was already on, in preparation for his return trip home. He walked over to the car and he again sat in the front passenger seat and I sat directly behind him, not to monitor him this time, but to give him the proper respect he deserved.

He said, "Bretta, I want my life to be just like that light up there on my porch. No more darkness for me. I want to shine, shine, and then shine some more."

Granny responded, "Amen, Brother Covington, let your light so shine." We got to the church a little earlier than the night before and it was filling up fast. Folding chairs were already being put in place as we got ready for the service. Granny sat in the amen corner with her amen and hallelujah friends, I sat with the teenage crowd, and Mr. Covington proudly walked in, removed his short-brimmed dress hat, and put his shoulders back as much as possible. He pimp walked all the way down the center aisle to the front of the church. Once he arrived, he chose to sit in the very first seat in the very first row. When he sat down, the church erupted in a roaring applause and you could hear several people say "Amen" and "Thank you, Lord."

People continued to flow in, but there was no sign of Pinky. I wondered what happened that caused her to go to the Dew Drop Inn Club after service last night. I'd heard it said that old habits are hard to break, but we just have to continue to work on them until we get it right. I was about to accept the fact that maybe Pinky had had a change of heart about being born again and living the life of a saved person. A sense of disappointment came upon me. That's when the double doors at Beauty Grove Baptist Church swung wide open and in walked Pinky with several people following her lead. Directly behind Pinky was the owner of the Dew Drop Inn Club and his patrons. She was excited and felt the need to share a testimony. She went to the front of the church and testified that last night she had stopped by the Dew Drop Inn

Club to tell others about her experience at the church and about her Lord and Savior Jesus Christ. She testified that she returned there tonight because she knew that her Savior was depending on her to help spread the Word and to lead others to Him so that they too could be saved. She said that the rewards of being a child of God were too great to keep to herself and felt compelled to share with others about His goodness and mercies. Pinky Dupree said that the Dew Drop Inn Club began to empty out when she told them that if they wanted to one day see their Savior's face, then they must be born again. It was at this time, she said, that the patrons began to head in the direction of Beauty Grove Baptist Church. Big Freddy-mac, the owner of the establishment, who stood about six feet and six inches tall and weighed about 280 pounds, turned off the flashing red sign out front and flipped over the sign on the door that reads, "We are open" to the opposite side that read, "Sorry, we are closed," then locked the front door as he mumbled to himself saying, "If they think for one minute that they are going to leave me here all by myself and headed to the pits of Hell, then they are sadly mistaken."

Big Freddy-mac said that when Pinky walked into the Dew Drop Inn Club last night, he saw a new and peaceful person surrounded by what appeared to be a heavenly aura. She was excited to tell about having Jesus in her life and appeared to be filled with divine peace. He shared with the congregation that he had felt empty inside for most of his life. He shared with us that he had a beautiful and loving wife and that they are the proud parents of three healthy and terrific children. He has one of the largest houses in the county with a three-car garage, an indoor pool, and a hot tub. He and his family ate well and every closet in his house was full of custom-made or designer clothes and shoes. He spoke of his fine jewelry and that he had enough rings to wear on each of his fingers and his thumbs, if he chose to.

He said that, even with the riches of the world, something was still missing from his life that he could not buy. He had been searching for years, trying to find peace, but it was evasive and he could not find it anywhere. He described it like when he was a kid putting together a large puzzle, only to discover that out of the 500 pieces, 499 are in place and the one piece that would make it complete was missing. It was gut-wrenching not being able to fill the deep, dark, empty space in his life. Last night, he said, when Pinky Dupree stopped by the club, and learned of him feeling incomplete, she told him that perhaps he was looking for peace in all the wrong places. It was suggested that he seek and depend on the Word of God. The evasive peace he had gallantly pursued for many years was probably somewhere collecting dust, waiting for him to come and claim it. Jesus is a true friend; He is a friend to everyone. Big Freddy-mac said that, after listening to Pinky, he finally realized what was missing from his life and that it was not hidden from him, but had been in clear sight all along. The piece he was missing was God and his mother had been telling him that for years. He said it's amazing how parents can tell a child something for his own good, but he chooses to block it out because he thinks that he is smarter than them. He looked around and spotted his immediate family sitting in the congregation and made his way over to where they were sitting. His wife and children were overflowing with joy as members scooted closer together to make room for him to sit with his family.

The congregation began to sing an old familiar hymn entitled "What a Friend We Have in Jesus," written in 1855 by Joseph Scriven, which is still pertinent today. It tells us from whom we get our help. The following are the words of the first stanza:

"What a friend we have in Jesus, all our sins and griefs to bear! What a privilege to carry, everything to God in prayer, Oh, what peace we often forfeit, oh, what needless pain we bear. All because we do not carry everything to God in prayer."

With the singing of that hymn, the service got started. Rev. Joyner asked Mr. Covington to lead us in prayer. That man sho'nuff could pray. You could feel his words. It was not the usual flowery prayer so many say in a public setting, but it was a downright soul-stirring prayer. His prayer sounded like a child in need, who was having a serious conversation with his dad. The prayer sounded like he was praying for no one but me. It was evident that others felt the same way about themselves. Church members and visitors were up on their feet giving God all the praise and all of the glory. The Spirit was high up there in Beauty Grove Baptist Church that evening. There was no music being played. People were shouting as a result of them hearing the Word. It was what they were hearing that caused the Spirit to stir their souls and not the beat of a song. They were pumped up and ready to hear more, but out of respect for the pastor, since it was time for the pastor's soul-saving sermon, Covington knew it was time to rein it in and closed out the prayer. Rev. Joyner once again preached about

getting our lives in order and the importance of straight-
ening up and flying right while the blood still runs warm
in our veins.

CHAPTER FIFTEEN

WHAT COLOR IS YOUR TICKET?

This was the last night for the revival and Rev. Joyner delivered a thought-provoking sermon. He spoke to us in the form of a parable, just like Jesus spoke to his followers so that they could have a full understanding of the message. Of course, he preached about being born again if you want to see Jesus face-to-face. He also preached about a tour group who had been preparing for a trip for a long time. The designated date had finally arrived and it was now time for them to go. They were told to get their luggage together and be sure to get a box lunch. They were asked not to push or shove because there was enough food for everybody and the cost was included in their fees when they purchased their tickets. The traveling group was told to be sure to get a sealed envelope from the man standing up at the front of the room, who appeared as if he was down on this luck. He told the crowd not to open or trade them with anyone. The envelopes contained tickets and an itinerary for the trip.

When their names were called, some of the people rudely snatched the envelopes out of the man's hand and didn't even say thank you. Others said, "Who does he think he is? I paid for this ticket and he has nothing to do with whether or not I open the envelope. Who is he anyway, looking all disheveled and stuff? He must be trying to hustle a few bucks by helping out because I know that the charter bus company would never subject us to the likes of him on this long trip." When the man walked through the crowd, one person pushed him and loudly said, "Get away from me, you tramp," causing some of the potential travelers to laugh at him profusely. Some of the travelers were concerned about how the man was being mistreated, but did not come to his rescue. However, there was one man who started to pray, and he said, "Lord have mercy on this man and I pray that you give him some peace." The man who had prayed so earnestly was told that his itinerary needed to be updated. He relinquished the original envelope and was issued a new one. The response from the praying man was "I thank you, sir, for getting it straightened out for me." The departing group was now told to open their envelopes and to take a good look at their tickets so that they would know which bus they were assigned to ride. The envelopes were opened; some had red tickets and others had blue tickets. They were told that they would board the buses according to the color of their individual tickets. Some of the people begged to switch tickets because they wanted to be on the same bus with certain family members or with their friends. The answer was an emphatic "No." They were told that they were in charge of developing their personal itinerary and had unlimited opportunities to modify it, but now, all of the arrangements had been finalized. When they went outside, the first bus had the color scheme of blue.

Everyone with blue tickets boarded the blue bus, including the praying man whose envelope was exchanged. The other group had red tickets and they boarded the red one. The unassuming man who had distributed the envelopes and had updated the contents of the praying man's envelope turned out to be the driver of the blue bus, which had a lot of vacant seats available, and was chartered to Heaven. The red bus was packed with standing room only. The driver for the red bus was a man they called Lucifer, and his bus was chartered to Hell. By this time, Rev. Joyner had gotten everybody's attention and asked a very important question, which was "If you were given your eternal ticket today, who would be the driver of your bus?" A loud gasp, then quietness came over the room. Rev. Joyner then said that he had been preaching that same sermon for a number of years, about being born again, but it seemed to fall on deaf ears that didn't want to hear the message from our Lord, Jesus Christ. He said, "You still have an opportunity to become a brand-new creature by living an upright Christian life. Your future, my friends, is in your hands; please listen, and follow Jesus Christ. The Lord is still waiting on you with opened arms to accept you."

At the conclusion of Rev. Joyner's sermon, the mourner's bench quickly filled up. Others who wanted to tarry got on their knees in the pews or on their knees in front of folding chairs. Many of them prayed standing, facing a wall. The entire church was in prayer and on one accord as the powerful Spirit swooped in. That evening, many souls were revived or saved.

Pastor's Observation

At the conclusion of revival week, Rev. Joyner spoke about his gratitude to the Lord for the gift of salvation that so many received. He made it known that he was overjoyed for everybody as he pointed out his old high school classmate, Fredrick McFadden, better known as Big Freddy-mac. He told the congregation that he, my dad, and Big Freddy-mac were cut buddies in school—as far back as elementary school—and grateful to God for the rekindling of souls. He described my dad as being levelheaded and intelligent beyond belief, except for the day he brought a snapping turtle to school to tease the girls.

Rev. Joyner stated, "Little did Daniel Jones know that one of the little girls he chased with that turtle would one day be his wife and the mother of his children." He went on, "Big Freddy-mac was always a businessman, beginning way back in elementary school, selling candy out of a pencil box. He had a good business going on until Professor Taylor caught him and administered a few taps with his 'Board of Education' to you know where. Even when my friend Big Freddy-mac was in elementary school, he was taller than most of us and almost as tall as the Professor. I once heard the Professor say that Big Freddy-mac was so tall for his age that he thought that he might be a descendant of a Watusi tribe of Africa. Well, do you think that stopped the Professor from carrying out his responsibility as principal? The answer is an emphatic 'No.' Professor Taylor did not hesitate to take care of business. Everything was considered to be a teachable moment."

Rev. Joyner continued, "Daniel, Danny's dad, and I were good dancers and loved to move to the music. One day, the three of us decided to go to the dance hall down there in Mullins. We knew we were underage, but we went there anyway. All of the girls wanted to dance with us. We were on the dance floor in matching outfits, doing our thing, surrounded by a crowd cheering us on by shouting, 'Get it, get it,' indicating that they were enjoying our performance. Some of the young bucks standing around became jealous and started trash-talking. Not knowing that we were treading on extremely dangerous ground, we started to trash-talk back. They could understand Big Freddy-mac and my street talk, but our friend Daniel had such an immense vocabulary he could tell them about themselves without using a single four-letter word. This really caused confusion because they thought they were being cursed out by Daniel in a foreign language, but they could not determine which one. Our foes were able to pick up on the second syllable of one single word, and it was the word "habitual," which means something that is a habit. One of them thought we had called his mother out of her name. They really got all roused up and became angered because talking about someone's mama is usually a no-no and considered to be fighting words. They continued to argue and we started making up words and using the highest level of profanity we had recently learned from an R-rated, bootleg movie we had secretly seen. The atmosphere was readying for an old-fashioned knock-down, bare-knuckle fistfight—

or so we thought, until one of the regulars at the dance hall, who lived across the gully, came in and pulled out a long switchblade knife and opened it in a fraction of a second. He was known as Switch Blade Harry. His face looked like a road map with many old scars from cuts and stitches used to close his multiple injuries from previous fights. In an instant, the ruckus had gone from bad to worse and great fear was beginning to set in as the crowd began to chant, fight, fight, fight, getting louder and louder.

"We were getting ready to rumble, unwillingly of course, when something at the door caught the clientele's attention. Then we saw some familiar faces coming through it. First, in walked Sister Louise McFadden, Big Freddy-mac's mother, followed by Sister Bretta Jones, Daniel Jones's mother, and bringing up the rear was my mother, Evangelist Neally R. Joyner. Oh my God. I almost hit the ceiling for I knew we were in big-time trouble. We lived more in fear of our mothers than the guys who became envious and wanted to fight. We weren't interested in taking their girls or in fighting anybody. We just wanted to dance and have a little fun. Big Freddy-mac, Daniel, and I were young, foolish, and in deep trouble. Our moms were upset and ran us out of that place. I've never been so glad to be run out of anywhere before in my life and I thank God for sending in his protectors—our mothers. Big Freddy-mac didn't catch too much flak about being there, because his mother knew he was not much of a dancer and thought he probably went there only to be with Daniel and me. But before they had gotten there, however, when it appeared that a big fight was inevitable, he placed his saxophone underneath the counter for safekeeping. Our homeboy, Big Freddy-mac, had been putting down some serious saxophone playing. He knew how to play all of the popular songs and played his saxophone along with the records as Daniel and I danced. He did not receive the gift of dance, but he surely received the gift of being an award-winning saxophone player. He was in high demand to play his sax and we were so proud of our buddy doing his thing.

"Tonight, we witnessed the gift of his salvation after he accepted Jesus Christ into his life. He gave God all of the glory and the hallelujah praise. Remember, he couldn't dance, but tonight we witnessed that he certainly can shout. I want all of you to hear the 'Word' and shout all over this place, if it is the will of God, even if it means having to replace the sanctuary floor. Hallelujah! Brother Big Freddy-mac, I'm looking forward to you making a joyful noise with your saxophone up in here. I'm requesting, if possible, for you to open up Sunday morning service by playing 'Amazing Grace' on your saxophone, because that is truly what happened up in here during this revival."

Rev. Joyner said, "Many years ago, when I told Daniel and Big Freddy-mac I had committed my life to work for the Lord and had been called to preach, they were very supportive and it meant the world to me. As many of you know, first I went to mortuary school and worked in that business for a few years. While doing that type of work, I saw so many acts of deadly violence that had been inflicted upon spouses, children, and the elderly. Young, African American men, especially, being brought in for our services caused my business to boom. After learning what caused the demise of so many of them, all I could do was shake my head about them being killed over such nonsense. A few years back, Switch Blade Harry ended up needing my services, along with a young fellow he had killed. They both went for bad and wiped each other off the face of this Earth. I thought to myself, *this could have been me years earlier for going to a place I had been warned about so many times.*

"I used my professional skills to make the two of them look calm and peaceful. They looked like they would never even swat at a fly, but there they were with their spirits gone, ready or not to meet their maker. I constantly prayed, 'Lord, have mercy and I pray that you give me the strength to make a difference.' That's when I was led to pray the commission of Isaiah, as found in Isaiah 6:8, which says, 'And I heard the voice of the Lord saying, Whom shall I send and who will go for us?' Then I said, in accordance with the scripture, 'Here I am! Send me.' That's when God laid it on my heart that I needed to be more involved in working with the living and leave it to others to work with the dead. While working with the dead, I realized that all I could do for them was to help make them look their best so that family members and friends would be pleased with how they appeared when they said their last goodbyes. I believe, when they took in that last breath, their inner spirit vacated the body, which had served as temporary housing while here on Earth. If they were not ready to meet their maker, there was nothing I or anyone else could do to help save their souls. Thus, I prayed continuously to make a difference, but struggled with the idea of becoming a minister. I prayed to God for His guidance and after much prayer and fasting, I became obedient and accepted His call. To-night, I am overjoyed that we are on the same winning team and honored to have God as our impeccable leader."

Rev. Joyner continued, "During this revival week, many of you confessed and repented your sins, accepted Jesus Christ's death on the cross as payment for your sins, and received Him as your Savior. He chose us to make a difference by spreading His Word. Being saved doesn't mean sitting down and resting on your laurels; on the contrary, it means the beginning of evangelizing for our Lord and Savior Jesus Christ." An abundance of people saying "amen" sounded throughout the sanctuary, indi-cating that they agreed with Rev. Joyner's observation and their mission.

Rev. Joyner was getting all wound up and continued to talk, acknowledging that he knew the hour was grow-ing near, but he felt the need to share, particularly with the younger generation, and to remind others about how, when he was a child, our community was truly a village.

"Back then we had a lot of support from our fami-lies, the schools, the church, and the community," said Rev. Joyner. "But nowadays too many parents become aggressive when you point out something that, if cor-rected, could help save their children from a lot of heartache and pain further down the road of life. Profes-sor Taylor had a saying about no more cotton pickers; be respectful and go to school ready to learn. Students lis-tened during those days and strived to do their very best. It's perplexing how certain people can make a difference in the lives of others, and I'm here to tell you tonight, we are those people. I'm so overjoyed about what God has done, especially during this revival, and I know he will continue to supply us with his everlasting love, grace, and mercy. I think everyone would agree that we need to re-kindle the village concept within our community and build strength and unity amongst us. Not just for us, but to spread the love of our Lord and Savior Jesus Christ far and near." Rev. Joyner finished his unity summary and invited us to the Fellowship Hall for cake and punch. He said grace, and the congregation was dismissed as we sang, "May God be with you until we meet again."

In the Fellowship Hall, Granny was talking with Pinky, along with some of the other ladies, welcoming her into the church family, and Mr. Covington was in deep conversation with some of the younger men who wanted to hear what he had to say. They were listening intently, hanging on to his every word. It was hard for them to believe that he was the same man who would curse them out just for looking at him. Everybody seemed to be engaging in conversations; therefore, I thought this would be the perfect time to talk with Rev. Joyner about a lingering question that was on my mind. I asked if it would be alright, when I returned home to my parents, for me to call his daughter, Phoebe, on her cell to keep in touch. He stepped back, took a hard swallow, and quickly asked if I planned to attend church on Sunday. I answered in the affirmative. He said that he would need to talk with his wife and Phoebe and would get back to me at that time. I had never asked for that kind of permission before, but I felt like she was special and that this was the right thing to do. I felt good and I did not need anyone to pat me on my back. When we were about to leave, I said good night and I reminded

Rev. Joyner that I would see him bright and early on Sunday morning.

In the car, the conversation was great as we headed towards Mr. Covington's house. We talked all the way there about the service and how Pinky Dupree had cleared out the Dew Drop Inn Club by spreading the Word. Granny said, "People have been talking about clearing out that place for years, and Pinky accomplished it in less than twenty-four hours. Hallelujah, talk about the power of God! She is a new creature in Christ and I am going to support and help her to grow. I know all too well, without proper guidance, how easy it is to fall back into sin. Often it depends upon who you hang around with or the places you may go. Sometimes even beloved family members can prove to become obstacles in a Christian's life. So, this old lady is willing and excited to accept a new challenge, to assist Pinky Dupree in any way God sees fit. She is going to need support—a lot of it—as she brings others to Christ."

When we arrived at Mr. Covington's house, the porch light was shining bright. He did not have a problem finding his way and said, "It's astonishing what a light can do. It brings it all into perspective." With those parting words, we headed to Granny's house and drove past the Dew Drop Inn Club. I asked Granny if she thought that Mr. Big Freddy-mac would keep the club closed. She replied, "People change and things change and, according to Isaiah Chapter 40, Verse 8, 'The grass withereth, the flower fadeth: but the word of our God shall stand forever.' Danny, when you give your life to God, you have a different way of looking at the world and I have faith and believe that he will." The usual blinking red light beckoning people to come in was not on and the parking lot was completely empty.

She said, "I'm glad to see that sight because, if you want to find trouble, go to a nightclub. Sometimes it will be there waiting on you to arrive. If not now, it will find you in the future. Unfortunately, trouble and nightclubs seem to go hand in hand, like a perfectly fitting glove. It's usually just a matter of time before mayhem shows up to do its thing. Please keep in mind what Rev. Joyner shared about himself, your dad, and their friend, Big Freddy-mac, when they were young teenagers. They went to the dance hall to have fun and to show off the latest dance steps they had learned. Some of the guys became jealous of the attention the girls were showing them, and they ended up facing the initial phase of what could have been a fierce, potentially life-threatening knife fight. That was a learning experience Rev. Joyner encountered during his youth and he never forgot it. Over the years, jealousy has been given the name of the 'green-eyed monster.' It can cause a lot of turmoil."

I replied, "Yes, Granny, I know. Mom and Dad tell me all the time not to get caught up in other people's insecurities. Nowadays, we call that being 'hated on' and, as for me, I've had my share. I've heard Dad say many times that if they hated on Jesus Christ, then they will hate on us too."

Granny nodded her head in agreement and said, "No one is exempt. When we envy others, it can cause a lot of hate. It causes hate because we start to compare what other people have to what's missing from our lives. According to the Bible, Proverbs 14:30, New

International Version, 'A heart at peace gives life to the body, but envy rots the bones.'"

When we returned home, we were both ready for another snack. We had old-fashioned molasses bread and hot steeped tea with honey, a small splash of unfiltered apple cider vinegar, and a dash of cinnamon. The taste of the molasses bread reminded me of the gingerbread men my mom made during the Christmas season. It was really good. I thought to myself, *The old folks got it going on. What else have I been missing out on?*

CHAPTER SIXTEEN

THE WIDOWS

Saturday

Granny's neighbor and friend from across the road, Farmer Walker, came by to visit early Saturday morning with a peck of white potatoes. He was distributing potatoes to the widows of the church and community. Granny thanked him and invited Farmer Walker to have a cup of coffee. He gladly accepted the invite. He said the coffee was very good, but a little piece of Granny's homemade lemon pound cake from the cake dish certainly would make it even more delicious. He requested that she place the cake on a paper towel because it would not be around long enough to be worth dirtying up a dish. Granny gladly obliged.

Farmer Walker was a tobacco farmer and he and Granny talked about it being time to gather the tobacco. He sounded frustrated about having a difficult time hiring additional workers. He told us of his blessing of having a bounty crop this year and his need for more day laborers. He first looked at me, then turned his attention to Granny and asked her about how much longer I would be visiting her. Her response was that she was not sure, but that I would certainly be here next week. Farmer Walker said he wanted to hire me to help with the gathering of his tobacco crop.

Granny answered, "It's hard work, but it's up to him." The only stipulation she made was that I could not hang the tobacco up in the loft of the tobacco barn for curing. She thought that doing that job could be a little too risky for a beginner like me.

We all became excited as we agreed on the conditions. Farmer Walker said, "Fantastic, you're hired. Years ago, I hired your daddy when he was about your age. He really worked hard that summer and earned the same pay as the men. You appear to be a hard worker too and I would not be surprised if you earn yourself a big check next week. My advice to you is to get a good night's sleep—you'll need it—eat a big breakfast, put on clothes you don't mind getting dirty, and be on time when my truck arrives at 5:45 a.m."

I said, "Yes, sir," and we shook on it.

Farmer Walker, who is also a deacon at Beauty Grove Baptist Church, seemed to get a lifted spirit. He then looked down in his coffee cup and up at Granny and said, "Bretta, I have a half cup of coffee left and you know good and well I can't finish my coffee unless I have another piece of that pound cake to eat with it."

She said, "Yes, I know, my friend." Little did he know, Granny was already a step ahead of him. She had another slice of cake waiting on a different paper towel. Farmer Walker finished off his coffee and cake, stood up, and said, "That was very good, Bretta." He then gave her a large bag of shelled walnuts, saying that he was giving her a head start on getting her supplies ready for her Christmas baking this year, and that he looks forward to eating some of those same walnuts in his favorite cake, her Japanese Fruit Cake.

He stood up and grabbed his well-broken-in straw hat as he headed to the front door saying, "I've got to be getting on down the road. It's time for me to be about doing my Father's work. I've got to get these potatoes on to the widows. I know how you ladies like to have some good ol' potato salad as part of your Sunday dinner, to go along with your fried chicken and collard greens. Also, I almost forgot that the dinner would not be complete without a banana pudding made from scratch and piled high with homemade toasted meringue." He thanked Granny for his light breakfast, saying it was exactly what he needed to get some energy fired up in him.

We walked him to the door as he went out to crank his old two-tone red and beige faded truck. In the front seat sat Zack, his old and faithful bird dog, whose coloring was similar to the truck. He turned the key and the engine did not hesitate; it ignited immediately. That's when Farmer Walker began to talk about his love for his truck, saying it was getting old, but the engine continued to sound as smooth as a new sewing machine. That was most important to him; just like people, he said what mattered was their inner spirit, and not their outer appearance.

He waved goodbye and said, "Bretta, Danny, I'll see y'all tomorrow at church, if the Lord is willing." We responded, "Yes, sir, we plan to be there." He then drove on down the dirt road in his faded, rickety but dependable truck toward the highway. The bed of it was filled with several pecks of white potatoes, which represented the number of widows he had left on his list to visit.

CHAPTER SEVENTEEN

THE GRANDLESS TOUR

Granny and I finished what had to be done around the house and I asked her for a special favor. I wanted to see some of the places she spoke about in telling me about the past. She agreed to my request because she had to go out anyway to the town of Marion. She knew about my cell phone restrictions; however, she agreed that I could take some pictures that represented a part of my ancestors' past. First, we stopped at the store at the crossroads known as Zion. This is where the man Granny told me about would make the late Saturday night purchase of the unsold fish for his family. We made a left turnand traveled down the road a short distance until we arrived where the tenant house Granny had lived in as a child once stood. Miss Ellie's house, with the inside plumbing that she'd had the pleasure of using once as a child, was replaced with a large modern brick home. We traveled for a few more miles until we reached the old school, which stood abandoned with broken windows and high grass. It was once the nucleus of so many fun activities in the community; however, it closed after integration. The school was built in the early 1950s to replace the old school where Granny's parents were students. Even though the new school was built out of bricks, it continued to be obsolete, with the outhouses still existing on the side of the school. As a matter of fact, the most memorable thing about the early 1950s school was that the newly constructed outhouse for the girls was not built for single occupancy like before, but upgraded—or so they thought—with a two-seater and no partition between them. How grotesque and humiliating. The older girls refused to share the outhouse when others occupied it. The teachers said that, since they were older, they needed a little more privacy. I took a picture of the old abandoned school and my heart felt troubled about how my people had to live like they were less than human.

Granny and I headed to the small town of Mullins. This was the town that many African Americans would go to on Saturday nights after working on the farm all week long. They would go to dance, converse, and have a good time and to check out who might have come home from "up the road" as they called it—meaning from up north—to visit. A train track ran straight through the center of town. African Americans would mostly be on one side of the tracks, gathering up on a corner, which served as their unofficial hub. This place held many memories, some good and some not so good. When disagreements occurred and ended up in fights, the fight would usually be the end of the feud. Today, however, things were entirely different. Too often, those same types of disagreements lead to severe injuries or death for one participant and a long sentence in prison for the other. Nobody wins; it's a lose-lose situation.

Granny pointed out the bank building on the corner, the restaurant where they were not allowed to sit down and eat, the dance hall, and the Five and Ten Cents Store. Granny explained that, back in the day as soon as African American people stepped foot inside a store, there would be someone there asking them, "Can I help you, ma'am?" Then they would follow you around like they were your shadow. One day, she said, her cousin Myrtle from up north had returned home for a visit. When she went in the Five and Ten Cents Store, as usual one of the workers said, "Can I help you, ma'am?" and started to take a step behind her every time she took one. She felt insulted at the thought of being treated like a common thief and decided to leave. But before she did, she looked at a ton of merchandise and asked the clerk to pull many of the items from different parts of the store and to place them at the front by the cash register. The clerk was very happy, as she anticipated getting a big bonus for making such a large sale. She even had the clerk to go to the back to bring out several pairs of shoes. Granny's cousin continued to make selections, some of which required the clerk to use a ladder, and others down low and all the way in the back of a variety of cabinets. She had a great time making selections and continued to make some more. Granny was told a second clerk was called to help assist the first clerk as she seemed determined not to let her out of her sight. Myrtle became tired of shopping and headed towards the front of the store and looked at the displays up there. She took her time and looked at more merchandise, then took three steps.

Again, her movement was matched by the clerk taking three steps. She then took one additional step and abruptly stopped and turned around so that the two of them were facing each other and standing toe to toe. She said that they were so close, she could smell the scent of raw onions and yellow mustard on the clerk's breath. The smell further triggered old memories of how she felt when she was a child being denied the opportunity to go in a local restaurant to buy, sit down, and eat something as simple as a hot dog with yellow mustard and chopped raw onions on top. She knew instantly that it was time for her to go. *How humiliating*, she thought. She pulled out her money, then reinserted it back into her wallet, telling the clerk she had changed her mind about buying any of the items and said, "I've decided to spend my hard-earned money where I'm treated with dignity."

She then took a few more steps, turned around, and defiantly flashed her money so the clerk could see that she had the ability to pay and didn't need to steal. The clerk looked puzzled but did not respond verbally; she just clenched her teeth. Her cousin was no longer that skinny little child who wanted to be treated with dignity, but now a tall and stout woman, who felt emboldened. She walked out of that store without spending one brown penny. She went across the street and got in her shiny, brand-new, long black Cadillac and drove away. Cousin Myrtle expressed to Granny that hopefully, as the clerk returned all of the items to the shelves, she might have an epiphany as to why she did not get a bonus that day. Cousin Myrtle told her that merchants need to step up and get with the times because her money is green wherever she goes and she expected to be treated with respect wherever she chose to spend it. The owner of the Five and Ten Cents Store's loss was another merchant's gain. Granny acknowledged that the clerk was more than likely following orders laid out by the owner of the store, however, her action reminded her of the person who had denied her and her cousin Myrtle the opportunity to sit down and eat a hot dog with raw onions and yellow mustard many years ago. However, the thought of discrimination continues to have a piercing sting. It's often passed down from one generation to the next and it usually takes the love of God to purge it from the heart. No human being on Earth was born prejudiced, for it is a taught and learned behavior.

There was not too much going on in the town of Mullins, but it was the place where in certain venues people of color were accepted as themselves. It looked like a place where time had stood still. The old train station, located in the center of town, closed many decades ago and was converted into a cotton museum. Granny acknowledged that the dance hall was always crowded and continues to be a draw for young people and others who don't recognize that they have grown too old for the present crowd. Granny stressed that this was not her kind of place when she was young and now that she'd grown older and wiser, it definitely wasn't now.

She drove over to the small town of Marion, which is located in Marion County. Marion was more accepted by the older generation as a place to handle business, and they would go to the local Piggly Wiggly grocery store to pick up special items like sliced cheese or bananas. She also loved to go to the local hardware store. My dad would always say that a trip to Marion would not be complete until she went in the hardware store to look around. When we entered, Granny saw some undernourished-looking tomato seedling plants. We walked around but ended up back at the display of the puny little plants. They had been reduced from $.99 each to two for $1. She seemed to take a special interest in them. It was Granny's thinking that next week those seedings would probably end up in the trash or in the compost container. She related to me a sermon she had heard some months ago about a tree that was about to be cut down because it had not been productive. A man was concerned about the destruction of the tree and asked to have a chance to nourish and take care of it. He was given the opportunity and, by working with it and providing it with the support it needed, it flourished. Thus, the tree was saved. The theme of the sermon was "Thank God for a Second Chance." She felt that nourishing and caring could make a difference in the production of the puny little tomato plant seedlings. She shared that the same principle could also apply to the less fortunate. She would often say, "Nothing beats a failure but a try." So she bought the plants to add to her garden.

Granny and I continued to talk. I asked her how I could recognize a Christian. She said, "Quite often you can tell a Christian by the way that person behaves and treat others." She told me about a lady who, after a serious storm, had a power failure in her home and was in need of some ice to prevent the food in her freezer from spoiling. She had gone to several places and all of the ice was sold out. Finally, still in search of some ice, she happened upon a gas station and saw a man getting a bag and a half out of an ice machine before it all ran out. The man, who was also in need of ice, insisted that the lady take the full bag of ice and he kept what was in the half-full bag. The lady said that she had a hard time accepting the man's generosity. She did not understand how a complete stranger could be so kind to her, knowing that he had the same need. However, he insisted that she take the full bag of ice. She reluctantly accepted it and thanked him profusely, then went outside to drive home when she saw a bumper sticker on the man's truck that read, "I am a Christian." She immediately realized that this was the work of a redeemed man.

It was beginning to get late and we both began to yawn. It was time for us to get back to the house to sort out what we were going to wear to church the next morning. She was a big believer in planning because it saved her a lot of time on Sunday mornings and kept her from being late. I'd been looking forward to returning to Beauty Grove Baptist Church. I wanted to learn the decision of Rev. Joyner, Mrs. Joyner, and, most importantly, their daughter Phoebe, about my earlier request.

CHAPTER EIGHTEEN

SUNDAY DINNER

I woke up Sunday morning experiencing a feeling of serenity. My mind was clear and I did not have hate in my heart for anyone or anything. I felt like my inner self had been purged of impurities, somewhat like the purification of the fatty hen. *Oh, how can this be, with me not hating on anyone, not even Miss Bertha Mae Brown?* I'd finally seen the light. All this time, Miss Bertha Mae Brown was trying to guide me to the path of righteousness. I thought to myself, this must be what they mean when they say, "I was blind but now I see." Granny and I talked about the realization of my conversion all the way to Mr. Covington's house, and then on to the church. When we arrived, Pastor Joyner was entering the pulpit, and Mr. Big Freddy-mac was playing "Amazing Grace" on his saxophone. This reminded me of watching President Barack Obama sing that song in Charleston at the funeral of South Carolina State Senator Clementa Pickney, one of the Emanuel Nine victims. Rev. Joyner got my attention and gave me two thumbs up. I felt happy about the decision and was most appreciative because I wanted to keep in touch with Phoebe and my newfound friends.

Sunday was a good day. It was also a good day for people to visit each other, usually after they left church and went home to eat. Granny and I had what Farmer Walker described as the traditional Sunday dinner in that area. She had several visitors and when they drove up close to the house and turned off their cars, she would say, "Get on down, and come on in the house. Go to the kitchen and get yourself something to eat," and they did. They were not at all shy about eating. I thought she had cooked too much food, but according to what was left in the pots and pans—which was nothing—she did an excellent job of estimating how many people would come by to visit and have dinner or a little snack.

It was time to wash the dishes, pots, pans, and utensils. The responsibility of being the head dishwasher can be an overwhelming task on Sundays around here. It's hard work to wash such humongous pots. They were some of the largest pots I'd ever seen in my life. Granny and I worked together as a team. I washed and Granny dried. These pots were passed down to her from her grandmother, who had a lot of children and needed enormous pots to prepare their meals. No one else in the family wanted the pots and she gladly accepted them. Granny said, "Everything has value, even the droppings from a chicken coop are valued as a natural fertilizer."

It was getting late and time to get ready for my 5:45 a.m. appointment the next morning for my first day of cropping tobacco for Farmer Walker. After washing all of those dishes, I was beginning to get hungry and wished we had some more of that food she had prepared for Sunday dinner, especially the food some of her guests packed up and took with them for their evening snack.

"I believe in taking care of family first," said Granny, "and I love to share with others. Danny, I know that you are a growing young man in need of a lot of nourishment, particularly during this developmental phase of your life. There is no way I would have allowed my friends to come into my kitchen and eat all of the food and not have looked out for you. I believe in planning and not making snap decisions. So, after you and I had dinner today, and before the visitors began to arrive, I prepared a large plate of food, especially for you, wrapped it tightly, and placed it down low in the bottom of the refrigerator for safe-keeping. This action permitted me to be gracious to my friends and not have to limit them regarding what they may have wanted. Danny, always remember, we're family and as young folks say nowadays, 'Don't worry, fam, I got your back.'"

The food was already on a microwaveable dish. Heat and eat was all I had to do. It hit the spot. I remember it being even better than when I ate earlier that day. It's kind of like a half-ripe banana. You can eat it now or you can wait until the flavor fully develops.

I went to my room and picked out something to wear to the tobacco field the next morning. There were several old straw hats lying around the house and I asked permission to use one of them.

Granny said, "Certainly, those are some of Nadine's children's hats. They come over here from time to time to help out around the house. They helped till the garden this past spring and planted most of the seeds. They loved the garden so much and would come and water it when it hadn't rained in a few days. Those string beans I ate from the garden and that juicy red tomato you chose for your snack were planted by the hands of those precious little children. It's gratifying knowing how helpful children can be doing for themselves and others with proper guidance. Of course, I gave them a small token of appreciation to instill in them that there is dignity in work. The only problem is they can't seem to remember to bring their straw hats when they come. So I keep extra hats around here and make sure that they wear them to prevent sunburn. One day, they constructed Napoleon Bonaparte hats out of old newspaper and thought they looked pretty cool until it started to pour down rain. Don't get me wrong, the sun is good; that's how we get a lot of our vitamin D. But too much of anything may not be in your best interest—hence the words 'too much.'"

CHAPTER NINETEEN

THE TOBACCO CROPPER

The time continued to tick away and I knew I had to get things in place for my new job the next morning. Farmer Walker stressed the importance of being on time and ready when his truck arrived at 5:45 a.m. It was bedtime and I didn't hesitate to go to my room, say my prayers, then jump in the bed. It felt as if my head had just hit the pillow when, the next thing I knew, old "Redcap" began to crow his head off with his cock-a-doodle-do, signaling that it was time for me to get up out of bed and to rise and shine. I felt like a sloth, but I did not hesitate to get up and get ready for work. Farmer Walker had given me an opportunity to work and earn some money and I did not want to disappoint him. He reminded me of some of the teachers back at my high school. You knew which ones you could challenge and those you better not even think about it. Farmer Walker was a nice man, but he did not play and when he said be ready by 5:45 a.m., I knew, without a doubt, he meant it. I knew I would make sure to be the least of his worries about being on time and made plans to be ready to go at 5:30 a.m. at the latest.

Today was my first day working as a field hand in a tobacco field. My job is called a tobacco cropper. In some regions, it's called a tobacco primer, which was the same job my dad did when he was a teenager. I've heard my dad talk about his days of being a tobacco cropper and when he did, I thought to myself, no way, it could not be as hard as he described it. Although my dad is a straight shooter when he talks, with the way he spoke about cropping tobacco, I thought he must have been embellishing the degree of difficulty. After all, taking leaves off a tobacco plant seemed to be a small task.

Farmer Walker had one of the more skilled workers, Willie Earl, take me under his wing to teach me which tobacco leaves needed to be cropped. Some of the leaves had large holes in them. I asked my mentor if those leaves needed to be cropped too. Willie Earl said, "Yes, those leaves are fine. A tobacco worm had a big lunch the day it got hold of that leaf, and I think I see the culprit working on another one." He picked the tobacco worm from the leaf and got rid of it. It was quite interesting to see. I had never seen a worm that looked like that. It was green and looked plump and juicy. "In actuality," said Willie Earl, "tobacco worms are known by different names. The phase they are presently in is the larva stage, preparing to turn into some type of moth. Be careful of those worms. Some of them will spit tobacco juice right on you." Willie Earl, who was showing me how to choose the right tobacco leaves to be cropped, was on the next row guiding me along the way. He told me to take off the leaves beginning at the bottom, and being that I am right-handed, to carry them under my left arm, getting a large bundle, then transferring them to the drag. The drag was a rectangular-shaped container constructed out of wooden boards for a frame and burlap material to cover the sides. It doesn't have any wheels so the mule had to pull the heavy loads from the field to the tobacco barn where the ladies and their small children would work to get it prepped for the curing process.

I started to get tired and fell a little behind the other croppers and Willie Earl came to my rescue. He helped me to catch up on my row and said, "You did good for a first-time cropper. I'm proud of what you accomplished. It's time for lunch, but most of us don't eat too heavy during the lunch break. If you overeat, it can cause you to get sleepy and make the job that much harder to complete. We've learned over the years that a cold Pepsi Cola and a half pack of cinnamon buns with raisins and that thick white icing on top fills us up and gives us a lot of energy to finish the job for that day. Then after work, except for Saturday nights, we go home and eat a big dinner, get in a rocking chair, and go to sleep." He was right, after eating the combination he suggested, I had a burst of energy and was ready to work.

The lunch break was over and it was time for us to go back to the field. Some of the younger men started talking inappropriately about women. Occasionally, one of them would say something and the group would debunk what he said. One time one of them said to him, "You need to stop your fibbing, and she isn't nothing like that and you know it. If you keep on talking about my cuz like that, I'm going to go over there and bust you square in your fibbing mouth. You're just upset because she rejected you, and with the way you've been trash-talking about her, I'm glad she did." At this point, my colleagues' tempers began to flare and the rest of the help out in the field thought a brawl was about to happen.

Willie Earl, who recognized that things were ratcheting up, spoke in a commanding voice, saying, "Now, now, fellas, that's enough. Put a bottom in it. You know a first impression lasts for a long time, and sometimes forever. The two of you are not setting a good example for Mrs. Bretta Jones's grandson." His words stopped the trash-talking right in its tracks. They all knew Granny and that she would not have approved of such reckless, low-down, demeaning talk about anyone.

It's Watermelon Time

The tobacco field is a hot place to be in the heat of the day around 3:00 in the afternoon. Willie Earl said, "When we get to the end of our rows, it would be a good time for us to take a break and burst open one of those juicy-looking watermelons we passed back yonder growing in the center of the field. One of them looked ripe for the picking and ready to serve its purpose. We've been working hard for a long time and we need to refresh ourselves so we can gear up and have the strength to carry on." One of them sprinted down the row to get one. It was so big that he had to roll it to the end of the row with the help of his feet. We ate the watermelon and were very thankful to Farmer Walker for keeping us in mind as he planned ahead for that day. He knew that there would be a need for the water in the melons when it was time for us to work in the hot sweltering heat. It was also economical for Farmer Walker. It cut down on the time workers would have to leave the field for water breaks, and the sweetness would give us a little boost of energy.

I kept some of the seeds, like the story Granny told of the African natives who were captured in the fields during the planting season and brought okra seeds from Africa in their pockets. I looked forward to planting the watermelon seeds next year in my mom's backyard garden. I saved enough seeds to share with Granny and my friends. It's a wondrous sight to see little seeds lift their heads towards the rays of the sun and develop to their fullest potential according to God's will.

The workday came to an end and Farmer Walker dropped me off at Granny's house and reminded me about the 5:45 a.m. pick-up time. I wanted to tell him that he need not come for me tomorrow because slavery was over and I quit; it was too hot for any human being to work the way we did under the blazing sun. I knew, however, that would not be the right thing to say to him. I'd made a promise and I planned to keep my word.

The aroma of dinner permeated the air; however, I was so exhausted from being a tobacco cropper that I did not even attempt to figure out what Granny had cooked for dinner. I went to the kitchen and spoke to her, then I immediately went to take a shower. I was exceptionally hot and used only cold water. I had to wash my hands several times with a strong bar of lye soap to remove a gummy substance that sticks to your hands when you handle uncured tobacco. The shower was exactly what I needed and I emerged feeling like a new person. I returned to the kitchen and Granny asked about my first day on the job. I responded that it was quite a learning experience and I definitely learned that I did not want to be a professional tobacco cropper for the rest of my life. She wanted to hear more, but I dared not tell her about the trash-talking duel. If I had, there wouldn't be any need for Farmer Walker to come up here tomorrow morning or any other morning to pick me up. Granny would put an end to that by having me write a letter of resignation thanking Farmer Walker for hiring me to work for him. I think Willie Earl handled the situation out in the field very well. When he spoke, they listened and gave him the utmost respect.

I talked with Granny briefly about the use of tobacco and asked about the purpose of tobacco worms. I wondered where they went when tobacco season was over. I said that my dad has an overflow of animal and insect charts in his laboratory but the perplexing-looking green tobacco worm didn't appear on any charts I'd ever seen. I thought they looked weird but if my mom was here she would probably use the word "different," in an effort to not be offensive. All I know about them is that they love to eat tobacco leaves. Some of the leaves had a lot of holes in them. I understand it's a natural part of the tobacco worm's life to eat tobacco leaves and that they would from time to time spit tobacco juice on you. But why do human beings, the greatest creation of God, imitate tobacco worms by chewing tobacco? Smoking, chewing, or dipping snuff can be offensive to others and a hazard to your health. I've been told that smokeless tobacco, which includes snuff and chewing tobacco, is very addictive, even more so than regular cigarettes. It appears to me to be backwards for man to imitate the lifestyle of a worm. The nicotine from chewing tobacco and dipping snuff is released when mixed with the user's saliva. It is not swallowed but expelled from the mouth in the form of dark brown spit. That's what makes smokeless tobacco look so unappealing to me. My mom told me not to be suckered into using e-cigarettes or vaping. She learned at a workshop for medical professionals that they are heavily laced with nicotine and the companies are trying to bait young people into buying them by using fruity flavors. They don't seem to be concerned about getting them hooked on nicotine. Their main goal appears to be making money at someone else's expense. Working in a tobacco field is no joke. If the hairs on my head could complain, each strand would have something to say. It was treacherously hard, laborious work.

Granny said she felt that my first day as a field hand would be hard work, so she prepared a special dinner for me. We had fried guinea, long-grain gold rice with butter beans, a peanut stew, and corn bread. She called the meal "back home food."

Granny and I had a good conversation. I talked with her about my concerns for Farmer Walker's poor mule and that it looked like it might be time for him to be put out to pasture to be cared for and to live a life of leisure. He had to pull that heavy drag filled with green tobacco to the tobacco barn several times a day. I asked if she thought that Farmer Walker would get a younger mule or, better yet, a tractor. She had doubts about him buying a tractor, being that this was his last year of being a tobacco farmer. I was told that a mule is the animal of choice to do hard work on farms because of their uncommon strength and their ability to pull a heavy load. She asked how I came to the conclusion that the mule was ready to stop working.

"Danny," she said, "your assessment of the situation with the mule reminds me how some of the younger people think that they know more about older people than they know about themselves. Most seniors know what they can and can't do and will ask for help if they need someone's assistance. People need to stop assuming that they know what is best for them. When decisions are made about seniors, they definitely need to be involved in the process. I'm sure you have probably heard the phrase 'Stubborn as a mule.' Well, that saying indicates that if a mule doesn't want to work, he will not work. He will sit down and not budge. Getting outside of the barn and beyond that fence could be the highlight of his day. In addition, mules are not so easy to come by." I asked why and I received an earful; the main reason was that a mule cannot produce any offspring as they are sterile. Well, then I wanted to know how they got here and the answer was that they are the offspring of a donkey and a horse. Granny said that a mule can be male or female but they can't reproduce and that it has something to do with the chromosomes. She said that she didn't have a good understanding of it but I could do some research on the subject or to take it up with my dad, given he is a zoologist. I knew that everything God created was supplied with seeds to reproduce itself and keep the world replenished. I wondered if the development of mules was manmade, designed for them to pull heavy loads, or if they came along as an act between a horse and donkey on their own. I understood that a male mule and another male mule, as well as a female mule and another female mule, could not produce another mule. But being that some mules are male and some mules are female, what was the reason why they were unable to reproduce? She answered that I was boggling up her mind and that she was clueless and did not know. But she did say that it told her that this was the work of God, who is still in control, and that she was not in any position to question any of His creations.

I went to the den to watch TV but I can't recall anything that was on. I must have fallen asleep as soon as I sat down on the couch. Granny called that being watched by the television and when that happens, it means you need to get up, go to bed, and stretch out to get a good night's sleep. Farmer Walker continued with his early morning pick-ups, and on the fourth day, I could keep up with the men in cropping. On the fifth day, I had a burst of energy and could outcrop all of them, and would gladly return to help those who were lagging behind. We had to go back to the tobacco field for a half day on Saturday. This was the day they looked forward to because it started their weekend of having fun. Many of them loved to socialize at the dance hall in Mullins. So everybody was working at a rapid speed to finish. The work for that day was completed before noon. We finished so fast that we did not need a lunch break; even though I was looking forward to eating a half pack of cinnamon buns, a hunk of yellow hoop cheese, and drinking a cold Pepsi, I was more than willing to give it up to go home early and get out of the hot sun. Farmer Walker was one happy man. He had been concerned about getting the work completed on time and he thanked God for answering his prayers. His focus now was on getting the tobacco cured and then taking it to the tobacco auction warehouse to sell it to the highest bidder. This harvest was extremely important to him for this is how he earned the majority of his annual income. He was happy for the bountiful harvest and I was happy for the poor old mule. Finally, in my opinion, he could get a deserved rest.

Farmer Walker dropped me off back at Granny's house and commended me for a job well done. He handed me my paycheck and I couldn't believe how much I had earned for five and a half days of work. He had afforded me a bonus for stepping in right on time to help accomplish his goal. He said that he can't tell people what to do with their earnings, but he hoped that I would put mine to good use. He also said, "Some of those same fellows who were out there in the tobacco field working side by side with you this week won't have a nickel in their pocket when they return home from a night out on the town. They would have worked hard out there in that hot blazing sun and end up basically throwing it all away. Unfortunately, they are on a revolving cycle of poverty. It's time for them to step off that treadmill and take care of their needs.

"Danny," Farmer Walker continued, "being a farmer is hard work. All sorts of elements determine whether or not you will have a successful crop. Always do your part and your work will not be in vain." He expressed his disappointment in the fact that all of his children moved away from this area and showed no interest in taking over the family farm or the timberland. Mega farmers, small farmers, and, in many cases, some people who never farmed a day in their lives wanted to buy his property for a few pennies on the dollar and had started to constantly harass him about selling it, to the point of bordering on intimidation.

"How insulting!" exclaimed Farmer Walker. He said that he knew one fellow, in particular, was always checking records down at City Hall to see if he did not pay his taxes. If he didn't, then he was ready to snatch it up at a bargain-basement price. "They must not know who they are dealing with," he said "I might be up in years, but I still got my wits. I'd rather give my land away than sell it to a cunning, smile-in-your-face thief. I know when someone is trying to fleece me." It was his thought that he had worked too hard to buy that piece of property to have so many unscrupulous people ready to snatch it away from him for almost nothing. He was seriously considering donating it to a worthwhile cause, with a clause stating that it could never be sold. He called this his "lock down and shut out plan," his answer to knowing he could help people and wouldn't be a victim of being bamboozled. His pride meant a great deal to him and he was going to keep it intact.

I responded to him, saying, "Yes, sir, Mr. Walker, I totally understand and I wish you well when you make your final decision."

I thanked him for giving me the opportunity to work for him and I went in the house to see Granny and to show her my first earned paycheck. She expressed joy in my success and added how nice it would be if I saved a portion of every paycheck earned throughout my lifetime. That would be great, I thought, but this time, undoubtedly, I was going to buy those new tennis shoes I'd been wanting for a while. My parents had said that if I wanted a certain type of those shoes, I would have to earn the money and pay for them myself because they were entirely too expensive for them to buy. One thing for sure, the dance hall might cipher off some of my fellow croppers' money, but I planned to have something to show for my intense laboring days as a field hand. Hopefully, the sight of those expensive new tennis shoes I planned to buy would serve as a reminder for me to keep my head in my books and to study hard as I forged towards my future.

CHAPTER TWENTY

IT'S TIME TO GO

Granny told me that my mom, my dad, and she had been trying to make an important decision about when they thought would be a good time for me to return home and they agreed that I needed to be included in the decision-making process. They had unanimously agreed that the time would be soon. Granny asked if that would be acceptable to me and I replied in the affirmative. She looked sad and that is how I also felt. At first, I didn't want anything to do with this place, which I called "a nightmare in the middle of the woods," and now I was feeling a little sentimental about getting ready to leave. The place I dreaded coming to when I was on that Greyhound bus heading south, now felt like home sweet home to me. But, on the other hand, I loved my family back home and I missed them a lot. Also, it was time for me to get back home because I didn't want to let down the members of my school's football team. I agreed with my parents and Granny that Friday of the coming weekend would be a good day to return. Friday was chosen because they wanted me to have enough time to properly say goodbye to my new church family and others in the community. This would give me an opportunity to attend Vacation Bible School.

Granny and the people of the community gave me a different outlook on many things I could never have imagined. They gave me a new sense of purpose and a sense of pride. However, and most importantly, Granny helped to instill in me a greater love for my Lord and Savior Jesus Christ. She is such a wise woman and I'm glad she shared some of her phenomenal wisdom with me.

Vacation Bible School was held for three days, Monday through Wednesday. It was a lot of fun. We had awesome teachers and were served great snacks at the end of class each day. Ms. Nadine's children were there, even Knee Baby. Mr. Gerald picked them up on the church bus. One of the boys brought his football and said if we had time after class, he hoped that we could play catch. He wanted to learn my throwing technique so that he could also be like "Iron Man Dan." Also, Phoebe was there along with other friends I made during revival week. On the last day, we had a church picnic after class on the church grounds. Phoebe and her mother baked a large sheet cake for the occasion. Written on the cake in bold letters were the words "SO LONG, DANNY...WE'RE GOING TO MISS YOU!" That's when everybody started teasing Phoebe and me, but it was a "good tease."

It was decided that I would return home by way of a plane either from the Myrtle Beach airport or the airport in Charleston. We planned to leave Granny's house on Thursday, to build in enough time to visit beautiful Myrtle Beach or go sightseeing in historical Charleston. I love the beach and I knew I would have a terrific time playing in the salted ocean water, a creation of God, but I thought about the many beaches in this world that I could visit in the future. Therefore, my heart chose the city of Charleston, for this was the location of the port where many of my ancestors arrived when they reached the shores of the New World. Unfortunately, it was also the home of the Mother Emanuel Nine massacre. I chose Charleston because this was not intended to be a day filled with beach activities, but a day I wanted to pay homage to my African ancestors.

Granny and I loaded up the car, and she drove to downtown, Charleston, South Carolina, where my parents had made reservations for us to stay in a luxury suite at a renowned hotel. The suite was huge, almost as large as Granny's entire house. It was on the top floor of the hotel, and it was called the Signature Suite. When we stepped into the suite, Granny and I felt compelled to take off our shoes. Its decor was decked out in white on white. It was perfect and stocked with everything we needed. Its attractiveness could cause you to want to stay there and forget about leaving until checkout time. We, however, were on a mission and had little time to accomplish it. We started by taking two tours. One was on a motorized trolley, and the other was by horse and carriage. We went up and down the historical narrow cobblestone streets as we listened to the rhythmic clomping of the horse's feet and watched the swishing of his tail to shoo away flies. This scenario seemingly put me in a place and time that my forefathers had known. The tour guide pointed out where some well-known residents had once dwelled, and the cemetery where one of the most ruthless slave owners in that area was buried. The mention of his name prompted different emotions by different passengers. Some stuck out their chest and smiled widely while others gritted their teeth and shook their heads.

We went to the marketplace and bought some gifts for me to take home to my family. Also, Granny made sure to pick up a token of appreciation gift for Farmer Walker. He'd volunteered to take care of her animals while she was away and to keep an eye on her property. She said that he was a good neighbor and friend and that they have been friends ever since they were students at Spring Hope Elementary School in Ms. Smith's class where they used to make mystery soup for lunch. She said he was the little boy who added a cup of diced sweet potato to the mystery soup and made it special. He looks out for her and she looks out for him.

At the marketplace, it was interesting to watch the ladies weave baskets and other items out of sweetgrass. They were beautiful and expensive. Some of the ladies had their little children with them and they too were weaving smaller items, such as roses, out of the sweetgrass. This was the beginning of them passing down their artful skills to the next generation because they know it's important to keep traditions alive.

While at the market, Granny bought seven buttons—one for me, one for Lil' Sis, and five for my Aunt Claire's children, my cousins EJ, Bryson, Khabir, Judah, and Asar, who live in Ghana, West Africa. The buttons had "Guess who loves you?" printed on them, and directly beneath that in bold print and upside down was the word "GRANDMA." I pinned mine to my pullover and put the one for Lil' Sis in my pants pocket.

We continued to walk around in the marketplace, looking at and admiring a variety of merchandise. I then noticed that Granny began to walk a little slower. She said that her knees were trying to spoil our fun but she knew exactly how to put that pain back in its place. She pulled out a small container of her rubbing salve and put a dab of it on each knee. She said that the pain had instantly lessened and her next words were "Let's sit down, rest, and have lunch."

We went to a crowded seafood restaurant. She liked seeing the large crowd because she felt something must be good in there if all of those people were waiting to get in. Surprisingly, we were quickly seated and she ordered the "Senior Citizen's Special of the Day Platter." It consisted of six large shrimp, French fries, coleslaw, and hush puppies. She also ordered a large glass of sweet tea, with a lot of crushed ice, and lemon on the side. She encouraged me to order whatever my heart and stomach so desired. That was all I needed to hear. I ordered the "Greedy Man's Platter," the largest entree on the menu. I had so much food, it took two servers to bring out my order. My drink of choice was a large glass of pristine water, a gift from the Heavens. We ate and talked and had a good ol' time. The server returned and asked about dessert. I didn't order anything. I was filled to the gills. Granny said, "Yes, I would like a slice of the praline and cream cake to go. Also, please bring out some to-go boxes for these leftovers." The server returned with the cake as Granny was taking out her credit card to pay the bill.

The server said, "No charge for your lunch, madam. It has been taken care of by one of our regular patrons and I want you to know that she has taken care of everything, including a hefty hallelujah tip."

"Where is she?" we inquired.

The server indicated that the patron left about ten minutes earlier, stating that she did not want any recognition. "She enjoyed sitting at her table and taking in the fellowship of the love shared between a grandparent and a grandchild," said the server. "She noticed you and your grandson when he opened and held the door for you to enter into the restaurant and when you were about to be seated, he pulled out the chair for you to sit down. She was most impressed with how the two of you talked, laughed, and enjoyed each other's company. The lady also said she believes it's important to have grandparents in the lives of their grandchildren. She noticed that there was something special about the two of you and how watching you put a smile on her face and joy in her heart. By the way, I included an additional slice of cake in the to-go box for your grandson. Enjoy! Please come back to see us again and have a blessed day." Granny and I were surprised about receiving a free meal and a double serving of dessert for just being ourselves.

Window Shopping

We left the restaurant and headed back to our hotel, stopping to glance at the new styles on display in the storefront windows. One particular store caught Granny's eye. It was a boutique hat shop that specialized in custom-made hats for women. I tried to encourage her to go inside because I wanted to buy her something special.

She thanked me for the gesture, then said, "Danny, this is a word to the wise: when you see the words boutique, custom-made, gourmet, or specialty shop, get prepared to pay a little extra. You worked hard for that money and I want you to be a good steward of it."

We decided to go into the boutique to just browse around when we saw a reflection in the window of someone standing directly behind us. It was the image of a man who quickly engaged us in conversation, asking if we had enjoyed our lunch. We answered yes, prompting me to think that he must have been the person who had taken care of our bill back at the restaurant; however, I recalled that the server had referred to the regular patron as a "she," so I knew that it was not him. It was even more shocking when he said that he was a long way from home, broke, and had not eaten for the past two days. Out of curiosity I asked him where he was from. He said that he was from a small town in Iowa. He asked if we would share a small portion of our leftovers with him. I was still stuffed, so I gave him the entire container of food and Granny gave him a slice of the praline and cream cake. He was most appreciative and thankful to us for helping him, then scurried away to a place of solace to eat.

Trials and Tribulations

I shared with Granny how the stranger's words of "being a long way from home" were haunting me as my mind traveled back to the journey of my forefathers who had once been kings, queens, mathematicians, physicians, artists, architects, and other very successful people in their own right. Many of them came through the Port of Charleston, which we had visited that morning while on tour, after crossing over the vast Atlantic Ocean. They were packed in ships like sardines in a tin can for months, shackled and having to wallow in their own filth. I read a piece of literature outlining some of their trials and tribulations even before they set foot on this shore. Some gave birth as they crossed that ocean, in inhumane conditions. The weaker ones did not survive from the shores of Africa to America; however, those who did were considered to be of stronger body and mind.

There was a lot they had to endure, from being separated from their families and loved ones, to learning a new language, and a new gruesome way of life. They endured being disrespected, with men being called "boy" and the women being referred to as "mammy." They did not have a choice about learning a new culture and having to live a subservient life as a people, for hundreds of years. I told Granny that I'd made the right decision in choosing Charleston. Granny's reciting of old stories, passed down from one generation to the next, along with a short but important visit to Charleston, gave me a sense of connection to my native land that I had never felt before. I could figuratively feel the rhythm of the drums from my native land pounding deeply within my soul. If

God could take care of them during their struggles, then I knew that he would take care of me. I was ready to commit myself to studying harder and to doing my very best at whatever I did. I was part of the new generation of a proud and resilient people. I wished that others around the world would learn that life for my ancestors did not begin with slavery. Granny agreed, saying we all need to know where we've been so we'll know where we're going. She emphasized that it was important to take the time to look back, but not for too long, because if we did, we might trip and miss out on a bright future.

We returned to the hotel, took out the clothes to be worn on the following day for my return trip back home, and packed the gifts in my carry-on bag. We talked as we always did about many issues. I asked her why it was decided that I would fly back home rather than riding the bus.

She said, "Good question, Danny; there has been a big change in your life and you earned this first-class ticket. When it was decided that you would be coming south, I recommended the slow, tedious bus ride to your parents, in order to give you some time to reflect and process the reasons why you were on that bus. When you first arrived, I must admit, I became concerned because my sweet little Danny did not appear to be so little or sweet anymore. The constant frown across your brow spoke volumes without you saying a single word. It was like there was a war going on within you. It was clear that a metamorphosis was in progress and was in need of guidance. I gladly accepted the challenge. You needed to get it together. You have always been a well-behaved child and, at this juncture of your life, in need of a little fine-tuning in the right places."

The Airport

The next morning, before heading to the airport, we got up early to have time to eat a full breakfast. Granny told me that, at one time, hot meals were served standard on airplanes, then they went down to peanuts and pretzels and, on some flights, you might have to purchase your own snacks. She advised me to always have some kind of food with me because sometimes you don't know when you are going to get your next meal, so be prepared.

It was time to leave the hotel and to go to check in at the Charleston airport.

"Danny," Granny said, "when I think of you, I think of that long poem you learned when you were in the first grade. Do you still remember it?"

I replied, "Yes, ma'am, I do. It is 'By Myself,' by Eloise Greenfield."

"Good," said Granny. "I learned it too. Let's recite it together as we go on down the road," and we did.

"Danny," said Granny, "I'm so proud of you and I know you will do well in life. I want you to remember who you are and whose you are. Keep your eyes open and always put God first in your life."

I responded to her and said, "Yes, ma'am, Grandma Bretta. I will."

On our way to the Charleston airport, she made an earnest request for me to visit Miss Bertha Mae Brown when I returned home and to do it without delay. I agreed and related that seeing and having an opportunity to talk with her was weighing heavily on my mind. It would be an opportunity to make right what was wrong and I knew exactly what I had to do. It took me going away for a few weeks to realize that Miss Bertha Mae was one of my biggest fans and was always in my corner.

We reached the airport, parked, and went inside to a kiosk to get my ticket and boarding pass. Luckily, I had TSA printed on my boarding pass. My parents felt the TSA mark would save me from any unnecessary hassles. I was glad because this was my first time flying without them. I gave Granny a hug, passed smoothly through screening, and headed towards the departure gates. I looked back to wave goodbye to my sweet grandmother and I noticed she had a wad of white tissues in her hand. She looked upset and I wanted to go back to hug her, but I felt it best to place my hand over my heart instead and said, "Guess who loves you, Granny?" I then pointed at myself indicating that the answer was "me." She lit up and managed to put a smile on her face. I reciprocated with a smile, then continued to walk towards the departure gates as I began to taste my salty tears.

CHAPTER TWENTY-ONE

BACK HOME

When I arrived home, it was too late to visit Miss Bertha Mae that day as I had promised Granny. The flight had been delayed many times due to bad weather. When we finally boarded and were about to take off, I thought of how I left home in an angry mood, but was now returning there in peace. It was about at this time that the pilot came on the speaker and apologized to the passengers for the delay of the departing flight, stating that at our destination figuratively it had been raining cats and dogs with maybe a few growling tigers and roaring lions thrown in the mix. This was his way of describing the severity of the chaotic storm. It was considered too dangerous to take off from the Charleston airport any earlier because landing at Philadelphia International Airport could prove to be detrimental. The pilot described the weather as nebulous and somewhat unpredictable, with severe weather outbreaks with pop-up storms and gusty winds.

He let it be known that his goal was to be like Harriet Tubman of the Underground Railroad, who never lost a passenger. "Flying a jumbo jet like this," he said, "carries with it a tremendous responsibility and it must be in capable hands. I accept nothing less than a 100 percent success rate." He then began to pray, after stating that he was well aware some people objected to praying in public places, but he was a man of faith and his goal, with the grace of God, was to have a smooth and successful takeoff and flight, and to make an unscathed landing; therefore, he was turning over the controls of the airplane to God Almighty and that he would serve as His copilot. He ended the prayer by humbly saying, "Amen," as did several of the passengers. The pilot told the attendants to check the doors and to get prepared for takeoff. As the flight attendants performed their duties, the pilot began to talk about how great it was to be back in his home state and that he grew up out in the country, in a small place about an hour's drive from Charleston called the crossroads of Zion. My ears perked up. The pilot said, "My fondest memories were when I went to the old Spring Hope Elementary School. There was a man at the school we all called the Professor. He would not ask the students what they wanted to be when they grew up; instead he would challenge us by asking what we were preparing to become in the future. Well, I guess you know what my answer was—that's right, a pilot. Ever since I saw a crop duster plane fly over the fields, I knew that I would become a pilot one day."

The Professor made a great impact on a lot of people, I thought.

Down the runway we went and up in the air as we headed towards our destination. It was a smooth, relaxing flight without a glitch and then an effortless touchdown on the tarmac, landing without incident. When the plane came to a complete stop and the "fasten your seat belt" signs were turned off, the passengers erupted in a thunderous applause and cheered when they heard the pilot declare, "God is good."

When I disembarked the plane and went to the baggage claim area, I saw my mom, my dad, and Lil' Sis waiting for me. I felt good all over seeing them and I was more aware of how much I had really missed my family. I told them about my promise to Granny to visit Miss Bertha Mae without delay. After some discussion, we agreed that the circumstances had changed due to the lateness of the hour, and that it would be best to put Miss Bertha Mae Brown's name at the top of the list of what I needed to do early the next day.

My parents told me to be sure to give Granny a call to let her know that I had arrived safely, which I did immediately. After my call with Granny, I asked if I could text Phoebe. My dad said, "Of course you can. Your cell privileges have been restored." I immediately texted Phoebe and stated that I arrived safely and would call her tomorrow. She responded with a smiley face emoji.

The next morning seemed to come quickly and I woke up early, even without hearing the crowing of my old friend "Redcap." His consistent early morning crowing had conditioned me well to get up early and Granny taught me the importance of being productive. I hopped out of bed and made myself look presentable. I picked up a jar of huckleberry jelly, along with a jar of muscadine grape jam, and placed them in one of Mom's special gift bags. I went to my parents' room to let them know that I was on my way to visit Miss Bertha Mae Brown. I told them that I wanted to go early while the street was still quiet so that I could give her my undivided attention. I felt that I owed that to her and more.

Once outside, I could see that I did not miss a single beat while I was away. There in her favorite window, on the second floor of her rowhouse, sat Miss Bertha Mae Brown. I felt a sense of uneasiness due to my past rude behavior and was not quite sure how I would be received.

I swiftly walked down the street, looked up, and approached her at the window and said, "Good morning, Miss Bertha Mae. How are you doing today?"

She replied, "Danny, I'm doing well, baby. I'm so glad to see you. You're a sight for sore eyes and, as we used to say, you look like 'new money.' When did you get home?"

I told her about the plane and the delays due to the weather, and that I got home late last night. After we had talked for a while, I paused and said, "Miss Bertha Mae, please forgive me for my rudeness towards you a few weeks ago."

She looked at me and said, "Danny, I forgave you a long time ago. I don't hold grudges, I love you. You're like family to me. Sometimes I see sparks of excellence running all through you. You are like a diamond in the rough, ready to be chiseled and polished. I just want you and your friends to be the very best that you can be and not get caught up in the ways and wickedness of this old world. Being kind and respectable can open doors you probably can't even imagine. Danny, I continue to be a believer of Proverbs 22:6 and willing to do my part. It states, 'Train up a child in the way he should go; even when he is old, he will not depart from it.'"

I replied, "Yes, ma'am, thank you for watching over me."

I told her that Granny had sent her a jar of huckleberry jelly and a jar of muscadine grape jam, along with her love. I then asked if she needed me to run any errands for her.

She joyfully replied, "Yes, please, I need some items from Old Man John's store. But before you go, please leave the jelly and jam in the doorway, then go to the store and ask him to add some items to my running tab." Her message for Mr. John was to send her a can of pink salmon—not mackerel, but pink salmon—and a three-pound bag of long grain white rice, a small loaf of white bread, and a large bottle of orange soda on credit. She said to be certain to tell him that her son would be coming home soon to wipe her debt off his books. I got my bike and rode to the store and repeated the food order and message she sent to him. He placed the items, one by one, on top of the counter, added up the cost, and wrote it down in his ledger book.

Mr. John said, "What about the onion? Bertha Mae always gets a large firm yellow onion when she buys canned salmon. You see, we go way back. I know her and she knows me. If you take this bag to her without that onion, that will mean that I will be seeing you a lot sooner than you thought, because she will say that you must have forgotten to tell me what she said or that I should have known to send one anyway." He picked out a large firm yellow onion and placed it in the bag.

Old Man John inquired about what was going on with Miss Bertha Mae and said, "When she buys canned pink salmon instead of canned mackerel, she is anticipating a very good day. Oh yes, you did say that her son would be coming home soon." He then reached under the counter and pulled out a small box with the words "Salvation Mints" printed on it. He put the box in the bag and said, "Tell Bertha Mae that there is no charge for the mints; they're on me and absolutely free."

I acknowledged his gift and message to her by saying, "Yes, sir, Mr. John, I certainly will."

I tied the plastic bag to the handlebar of my bike and pedaled back to Miss Bertha Mae's house as fast as possible. When I returned, she had closed her favorite window and had unlocked the front door. I took the food to the kitchen and delivered Mr. John's message. I said goodbye and started to head towards the front door.

That's when she said, "Wait a minute please, Danny, I want to talk with you about my son. You remind me so much of him when he was about your age. Do you have time to listen?"

I responded, "Yes, ma'am, I do."

Miss Bertha Mae said that she never married and consequently never had any biological children. But one day, many decades ago, a young child came into her life and filled that emptiness. She continued to talk about how that little boy would come to her house and sit on her front stoop for a few minutes every day, and often it would be during dinnertime. One day, he asked her for a special favor, which changed her life forever. That child asked her to be his godmother. She felt honored and gladly said yes to his request. Miss Bertha Mae said she made sure that her son got a good education and whatever else he needed—not necessarily what he wanted, but needed. She explained that he is a very successful man and that he travels the world working for the Lord. Even with all of his success and travels, he always makes sure to stay in touch with her and he often acknowledges his thankfulness to God for her presence in his life.

She told me that her son called a few days ago and said that he would be coming soon to take her home with him. She was excited about his impending visit and said, "When he comes, I am going to be packed and ready to go."

She continued by saying, "One thing's for sure, Danny, he will go fishing when he gets here for that is his favorite thing to do. Have you ever fished in a river?"

I responded, "No, ma'am, I've never fished in a river, but I've fished in small ponds at my Granny's house."

"There is nothing like it." She said the river is her son's favorite place to go fishing. She expressed her desire for him to teach me how to become a great fisherman. She said, "He has a bright shining light and he carries it everywhere he goes. Even when he goes down to the banks of the river to cast his nets, people and the fish are drawn close to him as he lets his light so shine. His light is a powerful beacon of hope. I'm so proud of him, as I am so proud of you."

Then she began to sing. I had not ever heard her sing. Her voice was tranquil and very soothing. The song she chose to sing, "This Little Light of Mine, I'm Going to Let It Shine," gave me a sense of confidence and encouragement. I joined in by singing, clapping my hands, and rejoicing with one of God's children, Miss Bertha Mae Brown, my beloved sister in Christ.

When I returned home after my early morning mission, I decided to sit outside for a few minutes to meditate and take in the quietness of my usually busy and noisy street.

Reunited on the Stoop

Within five minutes of sitting on my stoop outside my house, Damon and Marquise spotted me. They came over and inquired about my absence from the neighborhood over the last few weeks.

"Hey Danny, when did you get back home?" inquired Marquise. "Your boys have been missing you, man. It has not been the same around here since you left the neighborhood. Coach Blocker said if you didn't come to practice soon, he would assign the position he's been holding for you to someone else. He expressed his reluctance in doing it because he felt that, with your leadership, we've got the ability to go the distance for the big championship. Danny, you wouldn't believe how many dudes are lining up to move you out and are hoping you don't show up anytime soon. I also heard that a few girls want to get in on the action and try out for the quarterback position. They seem to think the opponents won't tackle them as hard as they tackle the dudes because they are female. Coach Blocker has been straight up with them—and everybody else who wants to be on the team this school year—that they need to get physically fit because we will not be playing tag or powder-puff football like we do during our spare time with the girls. Coach said that if the girls want to be a part of the football team, they are more than welcome to try out for a position. He stressed that once the players put on uniforms, everyone must be fit and ready to play. Our opponents across the state are out to win the big prize this year and so are we. We are going to play some serious football this school year, the real McCoy. Coach said he's interested in properly training us so we will remain healthy, strong, and off the injury list. He mailed letters to our parents and gave a copy of it to all of our teachers, counselors, and administrators at school. Letters were also sent to Old Man John's Store, the movie theater, bowling alley, and other places we patronize in the neighborhood, informing them that he will be checking with them to make sure that we are doing well. The areas of concern are academics, attendance, and behavior as there will not be any room for any slackness on his team."

Damon chimed in. "Danny, we've already talked and agreed that when you run that ball, we are going to be right there with you, my friend, like the Tuskegee Airmen were for some of the bomber pilots during World War II. I learned a lot about them this past semester. Before then, I didn't even know that they existed. They were a top-notch group of African American military pilots trained at Tuskegee University, in Tuskegee, Alabama. They were trained as bombers and fighters from 1940 to 1948 and escorted pilots on special missions during World War II. The Tuskegee Airmen were a tough group and their motto was 'spit fire.' These pilots were trained for aerial combat and were an example of excellence. I enjoyed learning about them in my Black History class last semester, as they are such extraordinary

African American men. They distinguished themselves from other pilots by painting the tails of their airplanes red. Danny, we want you to feel like the escorted pilots felt when they saw the red tails of the Tuskegee Airmen's planes shielding them high up in the sky. It is said that they made them feel safe, secure, and not alone. We are going to have your back out there on that football field. You can count on us. We plan to protect you to the best of our ability in an effort to keep you strong. All you have to do is to run fast—really fast—and we will take care of the rest. We're glad you're back home, my friend."

"Danny," said Marquise, "so much was happening around here and I needed to talk with you. I tried to hit you up several times on your cell to give you the heads-up on the happenings around here, but I couldn't reach you. Since you've been gone, can you believe that an anonymous donor gave the school 1.5 million dollars to use for the youth in this community? At first, we didn't believe it. We couldn't put our heads around it. Who would do that kind of thing for us? We thought surely someone was pulling a prank until we saw a story about it on the nightly news. It caused a big buzz around here with everybody trying to figure out who was the donor. According to the reporter, there were some stipulations on how to use the money, however, which were to hire additional teachers and tutors to help improve students' grades, have incentives to encourage good attendance, and to teach the youth about the importance of having good manners and respect for others. Coach Blocker said that nothing will be given to us and that we have to earn everything we receive. In addition, he told us that our old football uniforms are a thing of the past and he has already gotten permission to order new ones for the team. Hopefully, this will help to boost our school morale and inspire us to be the best that we can be. He also said that his goal is to make our school, the community, and especially our unknown donor proud of us because it was a great unselfish act that was given as an investment in the lives of our young people. He concluded his pep talk by saying someone saw our need and stepped up to do something about it. It is our responsibility to take advantage of the opportunities that are afforded to us. We must study hard, do our very best, and be proud of our achievements."

"Yeah, man," said Damon, "a lot has happened around here and I'm so glad you're back. Without you, our team would be doomed, and in big trouble. Nobody can throw or run that football like you, man. We're counting on you to lead us in winning the 4-A State Football Championship this upcoming school year. Coach said you're a natural and the best quarterback he's seen in his twenty-three years of coaching. He speaks highly of you and your skills, especially the way you throw that football spiral. We are counting on you, man, to help make our team more competitive, complete, and victorious."

Damon continued. "You look like you're in great shape. Coach Blocker is going to be elated when he sees the results of how hard you've been working out while you were away. Did you go to a special type of football conditioning camp to build all of those strong-looking muscles?"

Before I could answer, another one of our friends, Felipe, came riding by on his bike and stated, "Look who's finally back? Welcome home, amigo! Where did you disappear to?" I told them that I had been away visiting my grandmother down south because my parents became concerned about me being disrespectful to Miss Bertha Mae Brown and thought it would be best for me to go to a different environment to learn and to practice the Fruit of the Spirit.

Marquise responded, "What's that? How can a spirit have fruit? Are you certain that's what they said?"

Damon chimed in. "You mean fruit like apples, oranges, peaches, or plums that grow on trees?"

"If so," exclaimed Felipe, "I'm putting in an order for a few mango and persimmon trees! I have not had a mango since I left Puerto Rico about five years ago where they grew wild on the streets."

I told my friends that the answer to the Fruit of the Spirit question could be found in the Bible in Galatians 5:22-23 and recommended that they read it. Their responses were typical of school-age children—school was out for the summer and they already had a long reading list to complete before school resumed in the fall. Thus, they were not at all interested in reading anything else and didn't want to see another book of any kind. Felipe refreshed my memory that, for them, especially in the summer, the word "book" was a four-letter word.

We continued to talk, dance, and merrily listen to music on our earbuds, as we bounced around carefree to beats like energetic grasshoppers, jumping up and down, with seemingly no cares in the world. We had a lot to catch up on and the conversation came up again about why I was gone for such a long time. They had additional questions about the Fruit of the Spirit.

Damon asked, "Are you referring to a spirit like what we play around with during Halloween and call a ghost?" Felipe snickered at the notion that I could possibly still believe in ghosts and tried to persuade me that there is no such thing as a ghost.

"That kind of thinking," Felipe said, "is for scared little children, like your little sister, Marissa."

I repeated where the information about the Fruit of the Spirit could be found in Galatians. In addition, I shared with them that Jesus is sometimes referred to as a ghost. I told them that he is often referred to as "The Holy Ghost." That profound statement caused my friends to ponder why there was such a noticeable change in my thinking since I returned home. However, they were alright with me and the change, as long as I could still run and throw that football.

The state football championship was very important to my friends and me, and it was constantly front and center on our minds. Also, the thought of having letterman jackets meant the world to us because everyone could see what they represented without us having to utter a word. They were counting on me to lead the team in obtaining that elusive victory this upcoming school year.

We continued to enjoy talking and cracking jokes about each other. It was all gravy until Damon said that he had heard from one of his other friends why I was missing in action this summer, which was grossly false. I thought how amazing it was that some people think they know more about you than you know about yourself. Using my decision-making skills, I decided that this would be the ideal time to share my experiences about the past few weeks with my friends and to set the record straight. I told them that I had planned to share my adventure at some point in the near future, but believed that today was as good as any. I told them about the day I tried to run past Miss Bertha Mae Brown's house, knowing she would be sitting upstairs looking out of her infamous window. I told my friends that I was not in the mood to stop and listen to her old yackety-yak, so I tried to run past her house in an effort to avoid her and very regrettably, one thing led to another.

Damon, who was listening intently, stated, "Oh, yeah, man, sometimes that Miss Bertha Mae can be something else. She meddles in everybody's business but no one knows anything about her. Do you remember when the Genealogy Society Committee of Forever Grace Nondenominational Church became excited about tracing the roots of some of the older members? Well, a small group of members worked for months doing research on Miss Bertha Mae and they came up with absolutely nothing about her. They searched the census records and the baptism records at the church, to no avail. They also interviewed some of the older residents in the neighborhood. Each of them came up with the same answer, which was that Miss Bertha Mae has been sitting up there in that window as far back as they could remember."

Damon continued, "The members were in the process of doing research for the church's one hundredth anniversary program. They had their minds set on trying to found out Miss Bertha Mae's age and anything else that was available. They searched and searched but couldn't find out anything about her, even after using artificial intelligence. This defeat ignited rumors that she must be some kind of alien who had popped up from outer space with no traceable DNA. Another rumor was that, in her younger years, she was a mobster boss's lady friend and was in a witness protection program hiding out from other ruthless gangsters and that was why she was always on watch, looking out of her window to see if any of them were coming after her. All of that nonsense was fabricated in someone's idle mind, which some might call the devil's workshop. Nothing could be found out about her and the mystery of it spiked everyone's interest. One of the members sank to the depths of rummaging through her trash can. Nothing incriminating was found in it and she continued to appear squeaky clean. Miss Bertha Mae became aware of the invasion of her privacy and sprinkled the contents of her trash can with a powdered substance that, if touched, would turn your hands a bright red that could not be washed off with soap and water or any other solution. It would take a week or two for it to fade off completely. She kept this secret to herself. They thought it was impossible that anyone could have lived such an untraceable life in this day and time. We would see her day after day, sitting up there and looking out of that window in the flesh, but she did not have a paper trail. All they knew about her was that she took the time to speak to everybody who came past her house, kind of like a lot of people in the Deep South are accustomed to doing."

"One day," said Damon, "while I was helping Miss Bertha Mae with minor house repairs, two ladies came strolling by speaking cheerfully to her and stated that she looked so vibrant and wanted to know her secret for such good health. She replied, 'There is no secret, it's God. He's here for everybody.' She asked them how they were doing and they replied just fine, however, one of them started complaining about having somewhat of a challenge with some scarlet color stains on her hands. She didn't know how she got them and no matter how much she washed her hands, they continued to be a bloody 'red' color. This lady was so dumbfounded about her hands and shared with Miss Bertha Mae that she'd made an appointment to see her dermatologist. I bet Miss Bertha Mae thought to herself, 'So you must be the culprit who's been rummaging through my trash can, making a mess and scattering things.' She suggested that the lady retrace her steps like we do when we search for the origin of things, starting with the present, then going backwards, and the answer would be clearly revealed to her. She then told the lady, 'When you solve the mystery, please come back and share the adventure with me.' The lady with the stained hands said that she was thankful for the advice and thought it would be a fun activity to do and would definitely get back to her with her discovery."

The Colors of the Week

Damon reminded everyone that if we are not sure what day of the week it was, all we needed to do was look up at Miss Bertha Mae in the window to see what color she's wearing. Her clothes looked vintage and not fancy at all, but were color-coded according to the days of the week. On Mondays, she usually wore beige, and blue on Tuesdays. Yellow was selected for Wednesdays, and on Thursdays, you knew to look for brown. Green would pop up on Fridays with purple being her choice of color on Saturdays. No one really knew why she chose to wear certain colors on specific days, but that's what she would do. On the day she wore white from head to toe, you knew without a doubt that Sunday had arrived. That was about all they knew about her, except and most importantly that she loved the Lord. It seemed nearly impossible that this was all we knew about her.

Damon stated that his mom had spoken with members of the Genealogy Society and asked for a volunteer to interview Miss Bertha Mae to get the background information for the project directly from her. For whatever reason, no one was willing to accept the assignment. It seemed as if they started to believe their own fabricated lies and psyched themselves out. They became afraid of their own words. She concluded the meeting by telling the members that, since no one accepted the assignment, all the talk about aliens and the witness protection program rubbish, along with other theories they'd hatched up, had to cease. Damon's mother stated, "We never really know who we are talking to, or who we are talking about, and we need to stop, regroup, and be more respectful. I've heard some pastors say that, as they look out over their congregations, they don't really know who is sitting out there in the pews. The person you point your finger at or whisper about could be here on a special assignment. Besides, who are we to judge? I believe that no matter what we say or believe, 'God's got this' for He is in charge and He will prevail."

Jacoby

Marquise and Felipe then shared a conversation they had overheard from the window between Miss Bertha Mae Brown and Ms. Becky Genwright, Jacoby's mother. The conversation began by Miss Bertha Mae stating, "Becky, I've had an eye on Jacoby for a long time. You know I hold a special place in my heart for the two of you. I know you are also aware of what they say about 'birds of a feather'?"

Ms. Genwright replied, "Yes, ma'am, they flock together."

"Well," said Miss Bertha Mae Brown, "an old friend of mine stopped by to visit not so long ago. He knows I love to hear jokes and laugh, so when he comes, he usually brings a few jokes with him. Do you have time to hear one of them?"

Ms. Genwright nodded in agreement and said, "Now, Miss Bertha Mae, you know I always have time to listen to you."

She began the joke by telling of a man who had an exceptionally smart parakeet that had an extensive vocabulary. The owner of the pet shop had recommended that he buy a male parakeet because they tend to learn more words than their female counterparts. The man did and he enjoyed listening to his parakeet talk. Sometimes it talked so excessively, he would have to put a cover over the cage to quiet him down. One day, the bird's owner cleaned the birdcage but did not properly secure the latch. The beloved pet escaped and flew out an opened window. The man dearly loved his parakeet and desperately searched for him high and low for several weeks but could not find him anywhere. He finally completely gave up, citing that it was good while it lasted.

"The parakeet's owner," said Miss Bertha Mae, "was also a big hunter and one day he saw a large flock of sparrows flying high over his property. He retrieved his double-barrel shotgun filled with buckshot and fired straight up in the air. Some of the birds fell to the ground and he happily went over to gather his spoils. In the process of collecting the birds, he saw a colorful green and yellow parakeet with black markings amongst the birds and asked, 'Why are you here amongst these sparrows?' The parakeet, who was known for its large vocabulary, narrowed his response down to two words: 'Wrong crowd.'"

At first, the joke was funny, then I thought about Jacoby.

Miss Bertha Mae continued, "Becky, please forgive me but my conscience won't let me rest. It is not my intention to offend you but I feel that corrective criticism is in order. I've never been one who sees that something needs to be done and then waits for something to happen. I don't believe in waiting for chaos to erupt, then saying, I've known about it for a long time but I just didn't want to say anything. Over the years so much has changed and I can understand why some people, because of possible repercussions, don't want to get involved in the lives of others. But I'm going to step out on faith and talk to you about Jacoby. I've noticed a significant change in his behavior. He's starting to hang out with a crowd that does not do him any good. As a matter of fact, he's hanging out with an older group of boys known for dealing drugs and are gangbangers. At eleven years old, he probably thinks it's cool to be a part of them, but the truth is, they are using him to do their dirty work. They know that Jacoby can do things and get away with them because of his young age and they feel emboldened to use him because they are aware of his lack of parental supervision. If they did what they have Jacoby do for them and got caught, they could spend many years in prison. Please impress upon Jacoby that he is not UPS, FedEx, or the mailman and he's definitely not going to be their mule. He needs to stop being their delivery boy and let them haul all of that no-good dope themselves. Please rescue him from the grip of that gang before he becomes an engrained part of the system.

"Becky," continued Miss Bertha Mae, "please prevent your child from becoming a statistic of the streets. I'm becoming more and more concerned about him. His behavior shows signs of a child suffering from abandonment issues. Too often, he is seen walking up and down this street late at night asking the same question: 'Have you seen my mama, have you seen my mama? She's not at home and I can't find her anywhere.' Your absence weighs heavily on his precious little heart as he yearns for your presence. He doesn't quite know what to think of your constant absence just yet, but Jacoby is a very intelligent child and one day he will be able to put all of the pieces together. He is searching for the family he does not have at home and is glad to be accepted into any family unit, even if it means a merciless gang. Don't throw Jacoby to the wolves; they will destroy him. Take your child back and get a handle on yourself, Becky. I'm counting on you to be the great mother I know you can be or, one day, my dear Becky Genwright, Jacoby is going to make you cry."

Ms. Genwright said, "Yes, ma'am, Miss Brown. I'm already crying for the hurt he must be feeling. Miss Bertha Mae, it's so hard at times being a single parent and I thank you for making me aware of my child's situation. I guess I was too close to the problem to recognize it and I sincerely appreciate your wisdom. I don't want him to endure the pain of feeling lonely, rejected, and unloved. I know that feeling all too well because that's how I grew up. I'm going to make sure he knows he's loved, for Jacoby is the best thing that has ever happened to me. Tonight, I'm going to call his dad, so he too, can be more involved in his life. I love my son, Miss Brown; he's all I've got. It would be devastating if I lost him to a gang, the penal system, or to the Department of Social Services. I can't bear the thought of losing my child. Thank you for your concern and encouragement. I love and appreciate you, Miss Brown, for caring about us. I stand committed to being a better parent for my child."

Later that evening, we saw Ms. Genwright and Jacoby at the ice cream truck. She bought three large cones of ice cream. Jacoby took one of them over to Miss Bertha Mae's house, then he and his mom sat on their stoop laughing, talking, and attempting to eat their ice cream before it melted.

One of the younger gang members, Tommy, who was somewhat in training, went over to Jacoby's house, interrupted him and his mom's conversation, and stated, "Come on here, boy, you're needed down the street. Ralph said he's tired of waiting on you. He's got some business to transact right away. So you better hop to it right now."

Jacoby's mother stopped eating her ice cream and said to him sweetly, but firmly, "I'm sorry, but Jacoby won't be going down there this evening or any other evening. He is in for the night. Jacoby is a minor and any request for his presence must be made through his father and me. Please note that I said his father *and* me, not his father *or* me. Tommy, now get yourself away from here with all of that mess, and don't bring it back here anymore."

Tommy, the messenger boy, responded, "Ralph is going to be really mad." Needless to say, Ms. Genwright had spoken and that was the end of that conversation. As Tommy was about to head back to Ralph's house with the response from Ms. Genwright, police cars sped towards Ralph's house from both ends of the street. The young boy's eyes stretched wide open and he was so fearful of the police that he stopped in his tracks; he froze and could not move. Ms. Genwright ran over to him and directed him back to her house. She told him to shelter in place with them.

The boy could be heard saying, "Thank God for you, Ms. Genwright, and for protecting me from Ralph's house in the nick of time." Once there, the authorities put Ralph and his gang members in a paddy wagon and transported them downtown to the Philadelphia Police Headquarters to await trial. A padlock was placed on the front door of the house that had once belonged to his grandfather and, as time passed, peace returned to the neighborhood. Jacoby and Tommy became best friends.

Felipe then said, "Now let me tell you about Miss Bertha Mae and the girls. When they pass by her house with a lot of makeup on, she asks one or two questions, which are 'When did the circus get into town?' or 'Are you auditioning to become a clown? If so, I would be happy to write you a letter of reference.' When she made a comment to my sister, Carmen, she became flaming hot and was beyond upset. She told our mama that Miss Bertha Mae was always picking on her about her makeup and that her friends, especially the boys, tell her it looks good. Mama responded, 'You can't believe what everybody tells you, Carmen, and I'm glad somebody else finally got your attention! You know I've been telling you about all of that paint on your face for some time. You are a natural beauty and all of that makeup doesn't permit it to show through. You don't need it; however, if you choose to wear it, a little goes a long way. I wouldn't be surprised if those same people who have been telling you it looks good are sitting back, looking at you, and gloating.

Some people will tell you anything you want to hear, to get in your favor. If I had a hundred tongues, I could not say gracias enough to Miss Bertha Mae. Hopefully, you will listen to her and start looking appropriate for your age and stop sending out mixed signals to older men with your appearance. Also, I've heard you talking a lot lately about tattoos. You're not legally old enough to get one now, but before you do anything rash, please read Leviticus 19:28 as it pertains to tattoos in the Bible.'"

The friends enthusiastically asked Felipe, "What does it say?"

He answered that he had not read it yet, but he planned to read it as soon as he got back home.

CHAPTER TWENTY-TWO

MY GPS
(GOD, MY PERSONAL SAVIOR)

My friends and I scattered for a few hours, going our separate ways before meeting up again on my stoop later that afternoon. It felt like old times with the neighborhood crew back together again, with the exception of Damon. He'd landed a summer part-time job helping out Old Man John down at the corner store. My friends and I had a bond like no one would believe. We were closer than some biological brothers and stuck together through thick and thin. We continued to hang out and have fun listening to music, talking about girls, and engaging in a vigorous discussion about which one of us would get his driver's license on the first try. We were rising to a new level in our lives and believed that having a driver's license would give us a little more freedom and serve as a "rite of passage." Not surprisingly, each one of us chose himself to pass the driver's exam on the first try, which caused the discussion to come to an abrupt end.

That's when I asked my friends for their help. I told them that I'd heard a certain sound several times that day and wanted them to help me identify it. Just as I finished my request, I heard the sound again and asked them if they'd heard what I heard.

Marquise said, "I don't know what you heard, but my man Lil' Chris is pumping it up in my ears. You know they say he's a musical genius."

"And Drippy Trey," said Felipe, "he's off the chain. I love my music and I can listen to him all day long. My parents tell me all the time that if I studied as much as I spent listening to my earbuds, scholarships would be flowing out of our mailbox like milk and honey. Do you think I care? Nope! I'm going to be a famous rapper and I'm going to beatbox my money all the way to the bank."

I responded, "Y'all need to cut it out. I'm serious. Stop for a second and look towards the sky. Do you see what I see?"

"Yeah, man," said Felipe. "I see that awesome bright light. It looks like the power company is going to be charging somebody big bucks for using all of that energy."

"I hope that bill doesn't come to my house," exclaimed Marquise. "We're already living paycheck to paycheck and struggling to make ends meet. Some ladies from church came by today to bring us some food. I had mixed emotions about it. I felt happy but sad at the same time. But you know what, dudes?"

"What?" Felipe responded.

"One day I'm going to be rich," boasted Marquise.

The sound I heard, off and on all day, returned and we listened intensely, thinking it surely couldn't be what we thought. It sounded like a newborn baby, but then we decided it must be a kitten. We were not completely satisfied with our conclusion, so we decided to ride off on our bikes towards the sound to make sure it was not a baby in distress.

That is when Lil' Sis, who is very bright, energetic, and astute, came outside inquiring where we were going. She asked, "Are you going on another one of your unproductive treasure hunts like you did when you were younger?"

I responded, "We are going to make sure that a baby is not in trouble."

Lil' Sis, of course, invited herself along for the expedition. I emphatically told her she couldn't go because she was still limping from that horrible automobile accident caused by that drunk driver. "Besides," I said, "no girls are allowed."

Lil' Sis said, "I'm going to tell Mama. Girls can do anything boys can do. You need to get with the times, bro; after all, is it not the twenty-first century? Listen, guys, when a baby is born, he comes into this world with absolutely nothing, not even an instruction manual. He shows up with no food, no clothes, no Pampers, no teeth, and sometimes no hair. If the sound is a baby's cry, you need to take up a collection and go to Walmart to buy him some gifts and I need to go with you to make sure you don't buy him an electric toothbrush. Comprende? We'll hold on to our receipts in case we are wrong and we need to return the items."

I responded, "Welcome aboard, Lil' Sis. You know that we have to ride hard to get back home in time for our curfew. You've got to keep up with the pack. Can your leg handle it?"

"I'll do my best," said Lil' Sis.

Felipe and Marquise made contributions from the money they earned doing yard work in the neighborhood, Lil' Sis added money she earned helping Miss Bertha Mae clean out her kitchen cabinets, and my contribution came from the money I made working hard in Farmer Walker's hot tobacco field in Marion County, South Carolina. Gifts were purchased. The daunting question now was where should they go from there?

That's when I said, "I've got my GPS. Follow me."

Felipe said, "You got a GPS?"

"Oh, yes," I replied. "My GPS is God, my Personal Savior. I take him everywhere I go. Are you ready?"

"Yes!" everyone shouted. We traveled a short distance, following the sound, and came upon a tall building with a sign that had a few of its lights missing. The first word on the sign was THE. The last word was INN with a blank space between them. My divine GPS said, "You have reached your destination."

We went inside to inquire about a baby. The desk clerk said, "You must be seeking that young couple who came into town to pay their taxes. They wanted a room, but we had no vacancies. Go around back and you will find them in the tool shed. I didn't want to send them back there, but it was the best I could do."

As we approached the shed, a tall man stood in the doorway and stated, "I heard you coming. My name is Joseph, but my friends call me JoJo."

We responded in unison, "We are pleased to meet you, Mr. JoJo."

"Who are you?" asked JoJo. "Where did you come from and what do you want?"

We introduced ourselves and explained that we lived not too far away and that our mission was to help, and if necessary, save the life of a baby. We were relieved to learn, however, that the baby was safe, and not abandoned.

JoJo said, "I hope I didn't upset you by asking so many questions." He explained that he had to check us out because, in this day and time, one cannot be too careful. I have the responsibility to keep my family safe and free from harm."

I responded, "Yes, sir, we know what you mean."

"Come on in," said JoJo. "I want you to meet the apple of my eye, my wife, Madonna, and our newborn son." We moved in closer. The baby was resting peacefully in a cardboard box, wrapped in a towel with the word HOLIDAY boldly printed on it in green.

"Oh, come and adore our precious child," said Madonna. "He's so sweet, meek, holy, and mild. We love him with all of our heart, soul, and mind. He is a perfect gift. Our prayer is that everyone will love him as much as we do. His name is Immanuel. Bless his little heart."

Immanuel's gifts were presented to his mother—a Walmart gift card and Johnson & Johnson baby products, along with a frankincense fragrant candle. Suddenly, without warning, an almost blinding light came through the window. It illuminated the entire shed. We were overwhelmed and tears began to flow like a river. Sounds of unknown tongues filled the air. We all began to tremble and fell to our knees with our hands raised high in the air, giving God the highest praise, and shouted, "Hallelujah, Hallelujah, Hallelujah!" Then peace fell upon us.

After that blissful moment, I shook my head and stated, "Oh snap, where did the time go? It's almost time for our curfew. We need to get home. You know my pops is a strong believer in the Ten Commandments, especially the one about honoring your father and your mother."

JoJo and Madonna thanked the children for coming and bringing gifts and prayed for them to have safe travels home.

As we exited the shed, new creatures emerged (2 Corinthians 5:17). A conversion had taken place, and when we left, we began to talk to each other in an effort to understand what had just taken place.

Felipe said, "Man, oh man. I've never experienced anything like that before in my entire life. When the Spirit fell fresh upon me, I felt burdens being rolled away. I feel better, so much better. You know, I didn't do well on my report card the last nine weeks of school. I did not apply myself. I even failed Spanish, my native tongue. But tonight, I spoke in the language of the Divine Spirit which tells me that, with God, all things are possible. I'm determined to be a better student and a much better person. I still want to be a rapper, but I am going to study hard and become a well-educated one. I am going to rap in English, as well as in Spanish, and in any other language I learn, in honor of my Lord. I'm going to spruce it up and add a little swag to it. Bright and early on Monday morning, I'm going over to the school to ask my school counselor to rework my schedule so I can take one of those new foreign language classes they added to the curriculum after the unknown donor gave the school all of that money. I would love to rap in Russian or Mandarin, the official language of China. My parents have always told me that I am very smart, and who knows, maybe one day, when I am older, I might become a renowned interpreter, and with this projected success, I shall continue to thank God for His guidance and His steadfast love. I'm also going to behave like a lot of professional athletes do when they make it big—I'm going to stack up my money and buy my family a beautiful, large hacienda and help others who are in need."

Then Marquise said, "Whatever comes my way, I'll be alright. My Heavenly Father is the King of Kings. He is Lord of Lords. I praise and give Him all the glory and praise for what He has done for me. He takes care of everybody, everything, and every need. I clearly understand, now, why the ladies of my church brought food to my house. They saw a need and were working on behalf of my God. I'm so grateful. I want to be just like Him by helping others who need a hand up so they can get up. The treasure we sought and found today enriched my life. I am dedicated to working with the less fortunate and, one day, I will live in a mansion on high with my Heavenly Father. I'm rich because I am an heir to my Father's throne."

Everybody stopped talking to check out Lil' Sis. She started to walk around with a broad smile on her face. She began to tell about how her leg had been hurting for such a long time. She said that the car accident caused her life to completely change. She couldn't do the things she used to do, even the things she took for granted. "It's been very hard to fit in with my classmates," said Lil' Sis.

"When teams were chosen during recess or during my physical education class, I would always be the last person chosen for a team. This year, at the end-of-the-year school dance, I sat on the bleachers the entire time and watched my classmates dance, run around, and have fun. I felt so alone and they treated me as if I were almost invisible. I know that the accident was not my fault, but I had to suffer and endure the pain and repercussions of someone else's negligence. At school, they bullied me and called me many things, but the one that hurt the most was 'Big Limp.' It was funny to them, but it was not funny to me. It hurt so bad coming from them, because I thought they were my friends."

She continued, "Tonight, thanks to God, my leg doesn't hurt anymore. It stopped hurting when that awesome light came into the shed. When it appeared, I could feel something radiating all the way down from the top of my head to the bottom of my feet. I can walk straight now and I don't limp anymore. This healing has taught me that I was never alone because God was always with me and by my side. I'm going to rejoin the praise dancers at church and praise the Lord to the utmost for my healing. I want to tell and show the world what He did for me and spread His Word through praise dancing, from continent to continent, and when I do, I will leap and dance with all my might like David, when he danced for the Lord."

I stated, "My sister and my friends, you have shared inspiring testimonies about the goodness of the Lord. He is depending on us to spread the gospel so that others will be saved. We are new disciples of the King. By knowing God as my personal savior, I do right when I'm tempted to do wrong. I'm so glad that I have agape love, deep down in my heart, for everyone. It has been woven into the fabric of my life and I plan to spread it wherever I go, for Jesus is love and I love everybody."

Together, we lifted our eyes towards the Heavens. A rapidly flickering star had caught our attention. It paused and flashed once more as if it were a wink of approval from the Almighty Himself.

I took a quick look for the time on my cell phone and shouted out, "Curfew, curfew—let's roll!" Our curfew was quickly approaching as we scurried to get home. At this time, a very bright light rapidly shot through the sky. It looked as if it was going towards our neighborhood. When we turned onto our street, however, the light was gone. I wondered, *Could this be the bright light that Miss Bertha Mae said her son would bring with him when he comes?*

We were anticipating seeing and hearing Miss Bertha Mae, sitting up in her window, exclaiming, "You're almost late." Instead we saw the car of Rev. Abram Campbell, the pastor of Forever Grace Nondenominational Church, parked in front of her house, and unexpectedly, a white dove taking flight from the windowsill of the second floor. It flew diagonally across the street to the Forever Grace Nondenominational Church and encircled the cross on the steeple three complete times. It then flew due west, going just beyond the banks of the river as it triumphantly soared towards its destination. We were in awe as we witnessed this beautiful, magnificent revelation.

CHAPTER TWENTY-THREE

THE TRUTH BRINGER

The next morning, with deep sorrow, Pastor Abram Campbell announced to the congregation of the Forever Grace Nondenominational Church that Miss Bertha Mae Brown had transitioned from this world. He said that there was not a time in his seventy-four years of life that he did not know her and how she'd had a profound positive influence on him. Rev. Campbell spoke jubilantly and excitedly about their last conversation. He said that it reminded him of an exit interview from a job where someone had worked long, hard, and faithfully, but now eagerly looked forward to bigger and better horizons to pursue. Sister Brown acknowledged that she had completed her earthly work and was ready to wear her "regal crown," engraved with her name on it up in Heaven. She emphasized that she was not perfect and asked God to forgive her of her many sins. She continued to say that, after accepting Jesus Christ into her life, she knew without a doubt, that Hell was not made for her.

Even as a youngster, she enjoyed going to Sunday school and to church. That's where she learned so much about God and His abundance of love, mercies, and grace. She requested a festive homegoing celebration service in an effort that others might be saved and become disciples of Jesus Christ. Sister Brown asked that we be kinder and gentler towards one another, love the Lord with all of our heart, soul, and mind for Jesus is love. Her final words were to tell us, her church family, that she would be remiss if she did not remind us, if we want to see our Savior's face, then WE MUST BE BORN AGAIN.

Then, he said, "Sister Brown placed her tattered Bible upon her chest, gently clasped her hands over it, smiled, and slowly closed her eyes. This was when her spirit left this world in pursuit of a new beginning."

Rev. Campbell stated, "I began to shout 'Hallelujah,' over and over again, giving God the highest praise in appreciation for someone who had made such a tremendous difference in our lives, especially the children of this church and community. She shared valuable nuggets of truths with anyone who would take the time to stop and listen. Thank you, dear Heavenly Father, for having her on duty in our neighborhood for such a long time. We've been blessed by her presence and highly favored.

"There," Rev. Campbell said, "in full view, in the front of her family Bible, were documentations recorded by her maternal grandmother, whom she called 'Big Mama,' of family births, marriages, and deaths. That's how, in the olden days, we kept up with important dates and information. In large print, was the date of her granddaughter's birth, 102 years ago, describing her as a special gift from God and giving her the name of Bertha

Mae. Yes, church, our Miss Bertha Mae Brown was 102 years old and about to turn103. Her mother was young when she gave birth, due to no fault of her own, but the irony of this paradox is, what someone meant for bad, God turned into something good. The young mother re-dedicated her remarkable gift back to Him so her child could be a blessing to others. Church, get ready for a festive homegoing celebration service in honor of one of God's biggest supporters, 'The Truth Bringer,' Sister Bertha Mae Brown, an obedient child of our Lord and Savior Jesus Christ."

Granny and Miss Bertha Mae were friends. They met several years ago when my family first moved into the community. They hit it off like they were long-lost friends who had a lot to talk about. They kept in touch over the years and when she learned of Miss Bertha Mae's passing, she flew up to be a part of her fearless friend's homegoing celebration service. She said that, when Miss Bertha Mae was made, they broke the mold for she could not be replicated. She was very special and anybody who had the honor of having a little talk with her would forever feel blessed for having had such a rare opportunity. She loved music and requested that her favorite song, "Jesus Is Love," be sung by the choir and congregation at the conclusion of her homegoing celebration service.

A few days passed and the church honored Miss Bertha Mae Brown's request at her homegoing service. At the conclusion of the service, the joyful congregation exited the sanctuary singing her beloved song while they embraced one another. They even hugged and showed love for people that they did not know.

The Big Invitation

After Granny heard about the electrifying experience my friends and I had in the tool shed with the bright illuminating light, she started calling us The GPS Group. She was eager for us to visit her for a few days during our Christmas break. She felt that the passing of Miss Bertha Mae Brown would leave a tremendous void in the neighborhood and she wanted us to experience the evangelist explosion that was about to take place in Marion County, South Carolina. Hopefully, she said, everything would be well organized and in place by then. Sister Pinky Dupree, Brother Alford Covington Sr., and she had been dubbed "The Trio of Evangelism" of Marion County. Rev. Joyner had challenged them to put Marion County on the map so it could be known as the "Soul Saving Station Headquarters of the nation." We accepted her invitation without any reservation, of course, pending our parents' approval. She said, in addition to The GPS Group, she was prepared to sponsor an additional child, and asked who we recommended. Without hesitation, we unanimously chose our little friend, Jacoby.

I became concerned about Granny spending so much money, being on a fixed income and all, until she said that she once heard a pastor ask his congregation the question "How many Wells Fargo trucks, Brink's trucks, or any other type of armed security trucks do you see following behind a hearse going to a graveyard?" The answer was none. She said she didn't have a lot, but was willing to share what she had. My Grandpa Thaddeus bought some U.S. savings bonds many years ago and left them to her to use as she saw fit. Granny felt the need to help make a difference in the lives of young people, foreseeing their potential longevity as role models. She felt, by us spending time at the "Soul Saving Station," we could learn how to help others navigate uncharted waters. Too often, she said, young people seek out their peers, who might not know how to correctly guide them. Therefore, she wanted The GPS Group to be properly equipped and to serve in that capacity, beginning with the youth in our community and expanding to wherever else we might go. The U.S. savings bonds were cashed in for a worthy cause.

Time seemed to pass by swiftly and, before I knew it, we were heading towards the end of the second quarter at school and almost time for our Christmas break. Our parents were on board about us going to Marion County, the place I once dreaded going. Things had changed and I was excited about returning there on an official assignment.

Granny met us at the Charleston airport, and on our way back she drove us directly to the building that had once been The Dew Drop Inn Club establishment. It was the middle of the day and cars were parked everywhere. She was happy to show us the physical improvements made to the building and grounds, and how it had been turned into a center for the people of the community and the surrounding areas. The center had a lot of programs for the young as well as the elderly and everybody in between. Some of the programs included a day care, senior care, computer literacy, arts and crafts, health and wellness, secondary education preparation, and preparation for the world of work. Students went there after school for tutoring and other self-help activities. A young man formerly from the area, who had worked at a nonprofit in the state of Maryland, returned home to check on his elderly parents and was hired as the center director. Twelve people were hired to help run this operation. The deed to the refurbished building and the eight acres of surrounding land were donated to Beauty Grove Baptist Church by Mr. Big Freddy-mac. We agreed with Granny when she said, "There is no limit to what God can do."

We left the Community Center and headed towards the church. I had been wanting to ask Granny a question for a while now, but each time I thought about it, I would become apprehensive, not knowing if I could deal with an answer I did not want to hear. I've heard that when witnesses are in court testifying, lawyers don't ask questions unless they already know the answer. The question I was about to ask had been eating at me since I saw our beautiful bronze-colored turkey on Thanksgiving Day, sitting on a platter in the middle of our dining room table. Thanksgiving had passed a few weeks earlier and I know that, in this area, a capon was preferred over a turkey as the main entrée for that holiday. I had to know about my friend "Redcap," so I mustered up the energy to ask how he was doing.

She said, "Oh, he's doing just fine, Danny. He's still strutting around the barnyard and being in charge." When she answered about his status, I felt a sense of relief and wished I had asked her earlier about him as it could have saved me a bit of distress.

It was Saturday afternoon and our second stop would be at Beauty Grove Baptist Church, a pillar of the community, where we were greeted and treated like rock stars—that is, of course, rock stars for our Lord and Savior Jesus Christ.

Granny had spread the word of our impending visit and, when we arrived, it was an exhilarating experience. My buddies and I had won the 4-A Division State Football Championship and proudly wore our letterman jackets. Jacoby had become the water boy for the football team and did a great job. He also earned a jacket.

In addition to seeing the familiar faces of those I had made friends with while there last summer—such as Rev. and Mrs. Joyner and, of course, their beautiful and most magnificent daughter, Phoebe—to my surprise, I saw the bus driver from my earlier trip to Marion County and also standing in the crowd was my seatmate, Mr. Funky Broadway himself. In addition, other passengers who accompanied me on the bus were there: the little retired caring nurse and the lady with the crying baby and three other little children, as was the hallelujah server from the seafood restaurant, and the homeless and hungry man from Iowa, who Granny and I met while visiting Charleston a few months ago. I looked over to the right and there was the praying pilot, a man of faith, who safely landed the jumbo jet at the Philadelphia International Airport and joyfully declared, "God is good." I heard a dog yapping. I looked down and there, wagging his tail vibrantly, was the little black and white stray dog I had befriended from my neighborhood. I acknowledged him by gently patting him on his head and said, "Hi, little buddy, what's up?" I then paused to clear my head and to focus as I wondered if this was serendipity or a divine intervention sent forth by God. The thought of seeing all of them brought back memories of my beloved Miss Bertha Mae Brown, memories I now cherished. She would often say, "We may never know why God put certain people and certain things in our lives, but He certainly does."

Granny told us that the "Trio of Evangelism's" main mission was to teach us, along with other representatives from across the nation, how to sow the seeds of the Spirit, which would take hold and develop into the Fruit of the Spirit. The Fruits of the Spirit are love, joy, peace, patience, kindness, goodness, faithfulness, gentleness, and self-control.

My friends and I learned by no means were the participants of this Gospel Explosion Workshop perfect because some of us had to work at it a little harder than others to get it right, and when things got a little challenging, we refrained from throwing our hands up in the air and saying, "I quit." No, no, we just kept on working and kept on striving to improve. At one time or another, we will all find ourselves in situations when we will need a helping hand to achieve our goals. That's called being a human being. We were overjoyed, however, to be members of a team dedicated to help direct the paths of our families, friends, and others to Jesus Christ. A team where special attire, like our letterman's jackets, or certain words won't be necessary as we will be known by the Fruit of our Spirit. This will be done through evangelism, the spreading of God's Holy Word, which is open to everyone and is absolutely free.

Everybody loves a winner and wants to be on the winning team. Therefore, we are going all the way to VICTORY with Jesus. This dynamic team was led by none other than the champion of all championships, for He is THE GREAT I AM!

THE END (or is it a journey to new beginnings?)

CPSIA information can be obtained
at www.ICGtesting.com
Printed in the USA
BVHW032307140821
613885BV00002B/11